NO
PARKING
ANY
TIME

The Predator

Even the book morphs!
Flip the pages
and check it out!

Look for other ANIMORPHS®
titles by K.A. Applegate:

#1 The Invasion
#2 The Visitor
#3 The Encounter
#4 The Message
#5 The Predator
#6 The Capture
#7 The Stranger
#8 The Alien
#9 The Secret
#10 The Android
#11 The Forgotten
#12 The Reaction
#13 The Change
#14 The Unknown
#15 The Escape
#16 The Warning
#17 The Underground

<MEGAMORPHS>
#1 The Andalite's Gift

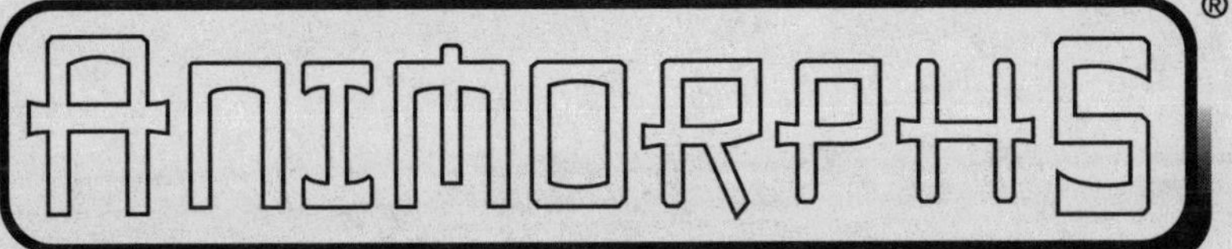

The Predator

K.A. Applegate

SCHOLASTIC INC.
New York Toronto London Auckland Sydney

Quote from pg. 59 of JOURNEY TO THE ANTS by Bert Holldobler and Edward O. Wilson. Copyright © 1994 by Bert Holldobler and Edward O. Wilson. Reprinted by permission of Harvard University Press.

Cover illustration by David B. Mattingly.

ISBN 0-590-62981-6

12 11 8 9/9 0 1/0

Printed in the U.S.A. 40

First Scholastic printing, December 1996

For Michael

CHAPTER 1

My name is Marco.

I can't tell you my last name or where I live. Believe me, I wish I could. I would like nothing more than to be able to tell you my name is Marco Jones or Williams or Vasquez or Brown or Anderson or McCain.

Marco McCain. Has kind of a nice sound, doesn't it?

But McCain's not my last name. I'm not even going to swear to you that *Marco* is my first name. See, I'm hoping to live a while longer. I'm not going to make it any easier for the Yeerks to find me.

I live in a paranoid world. But just because I'm paranoid doesn't mean I don't have enemies.

I have *real* enemies. Enemies that would freeze your blood if you only knew.

So, see, I'd like to tell you my name, and address, and phone number, too, because if I could do that, it would mean I no longer had any enemies. It would mean my life was normal again. It would mean I could go back to minding my own business.

I believe in minding my own business.

Which is why what happened on my way home from the 7-Eleven was so dumb.

I was walking down the street with some low-fat milk, a loaf of bread, and a bag of peanut M&M's. Since my mom died, I've gotten stuck with a lot of the shopping and stuff for my dad and me.

This 7-Eleven isn't in the greatest neighborhood, so I was walking kind of fast, minding my own business, trying not to think about the fact that it was after ten at night.

Then I heard it.

"Just don't hurt me, just don't hurt me."

It was a man's voice. An old man, from the sound of it. It was coming from a dark alley.

I hesitated. I stopped. I pressed myself back against the cold brick wall of the building and listened.

"Just gimme the money, old man, don't make

me hurt you," a second voice said. A younger voice. A tough voice.

"I gave you all of it!" the old man cried.

Then the punk said something I can't repeat. Basically, he was getting ready to pound the old man. I heard other voices. Three punks total. It didn't look good for the old man.

"This is totally *not* your problem, Marco," I told myself. "Stay out of it. Don't be an idiot."

Three punks. Each of them probably twice as big as I was. I'm not exactly Arnold Schwarzenegger. I'm not even average height for my age, although I make up for it by being incredibly cute.

And charming. And witty. And modest.

But I was pretty sure the three big gang members in that alley were not going to be very impressed by my cuteness.

Fortunately, I have other abilities.

It had been a while since I had done this particular morph, but as I concentrated, I could feel it coming back. I slipped into the opening of the alley and hid in the shadow of a very smelly Dumpster.

The first thing that happened was the fur. It sprouted quickly from my arms and legs and all down my body. Thick, rough, ragged, black fur. It grew long on my arms and back and head. It was shorter everywhere else.

My jaw bulged forward. I could hear the bones in my jaw grind as they stretched and the nonhuman DNA changed my body.

Morphing doesn't hurt. It creeps you out sometimes, but it doesn't hurt. And as morphs go, this one wasn't bad. I mean, I still got to keep all my usual arms and legs and stuff. Not like when I morphed into an osprey. Or a dolphin. I mean, when I was a dolphin, I was breathing through a hole in the back of my neck.

With this morph I had arms, as usual. Only they were a lot bigger. A *lot* bigger. My legs bent forward. My shoulders grew so massive it was like having a couple of pigs sitting on my back. I also had an enormous round belly and a leathery chest.

My face was a black, bulging, rubbery mask, and my eyes were practically invisible beneath my heavy brow.

I had become a gorilla.

Now, here's the thing about gorillas. They are the sweetest animals around. If you leave them alone they will mostly just sit and eat leaves all day.

And that's all the gorilla mind really wanted to do right then — eat some leaves, maybe a nice piece of fruit.

But I was in that head, too, along with the gorilla's instincts. And I had decided to teach those punks a little lesson. See, now that I was in that gorilla body, I weighed four hundred pounds. And I was mighty strong.

How strong? Let me put it this way. Compared to a gorilla, a human being is made out of toothpicks. I wasn't just twice as strong as a man, I was maybe four, five, six times stronger.

Further down the alley, the punks had lost patience with the old man.

"Let's just kick his butt," one of the geniuses said.

That's when I decided to say hello. To get their attention, I picked up the Dumpster and threw it against the far wall of the alley.

Yes, a full-sized Dumpster.

CRASH! BOOM!

"What was that?"

"Look! What *is* that thing?"

"Whoa! That's some kind of a . . . of a monkey!"

Monkey! I thought. *Excuse me? Monkey? I'll show you monkey.*

Before they could decide what to do, I charged. Knuckles scraping the dirty ground, small hind legs propelling me forward, I charged.

If the punks had had any sense, they would have run.

They didn't.

"Get it!" one yelled.

I grabbed him around his arm with one massive fist. I lifted him straight off the ground and threw him over my shoulder.

"Aaaaaaahhhhh!"

BOOMPH!

He landed on the ground behind me. The other two rushed at me, one on the left, one on the right. I saw a knife glittering. The knife slashed my arm. It almost hurt.

"Hoo hoo hrrraaawwwrr!" I yelled, in pure gorilla.

With my injured arm, I landed a backhand blow to the knife guy's chest. He flew back. I mean, *flew.* He hit the wall and dropped.

I just grabbed the third guy by the shirt collar and threw him into the Dumpster.

"Don't kill meeeee!" he cried as he sailed through the air.

I had no intention of killing anyone. I hoisted the knife guy into the Dumpster with his friend. He wasn't breathing real well, but I figured he'd survive.

Hah, I thought. *Who needs Spiderman, when Marco is on the case?*

While I was telling myself just how cool I was, I heard the sound.

It was a click. Two clicks, actually. The sound of an automatic pistol being cocked.

I spun around.

BLAM! BLAM!

It was the first guy. The one I'd thrown over my shoulder. He was up on his feet, gun pointed.

I was big. I was powerful. But a gun was a whole different story. And loud! Man, are those things loud.

"Hah! Come and get some, monkey man!"

I barreled behind the Dumpster. I leaned my massive shoulders into it and sent it rolling and spinning and sliding at the guy with the gun.

"Ahhhhh!"

BLAMPH!

So much for the guy with the gun.

I checked. He was alive. He wasn't happy, but he was alive. The gun was nowhere to be seen.

Well, Marco, I thought, *that went okay. Now, find someplace private, demorph, call 911 to come arrest these guys, and you can still get home in time to watch* Letterman.

Unfortunately, I had forgotten one thing.

"G-g-get out of here you . . . you *monster*!"

The old man. The one I had risked my life to save. He was standing, facing me. He was shaking with fear and red in the face.

Oh, I thought. *So* that's *where the gun went.*

The old man was pointing the gun at me.

"Back, you demon! Don't come any closer."

BLAM! BLAM! BLAM!

I tore out of the alley with bullets whizzing through the air.

Which just goes to show you why you should never get involved in other people's problems.

CHAPTER 2

"Yeah, so then I do the gorilla thing, right? I save the old man. I'm the hero. I *am* Spiderman. I *am* Wolverine. I *am* Batman —"

"Or at least Gorilla Boy," Rachel interrupted.

She did a forward flip as we walked across the springy grass. Rachel's into gymnastics. It's very distracting when someone flips while they're talking to you.

It was the day after my big hero act. We were all out in a far meadow of Cassie's farm — me, Jake, Cassie, and Rachel, strolling through little bunches of wildflowers. Tobias was flying overhead, about a hundred feet up, in a sky dotted with bright, white clouds.

"And what happens as I am playing Captain

America?" I ask. "The old man unloads the gun at me. I totally lost the milk and my bag of M&M's."

Jake gave me a disgruntled look. "Marco? It was good of you to rescue the old man. But you really shouldn't be turning into a gorilla."

Now, as you're reading this, you're probably thinking, *Um, Marco? Time out. You've left out a few things. Like, how can you turn into a gorilla?*

Good question.

It happened on a dark night when we were all heading home from the mall. There were five of us.

Me, you already know.

Jake is my best friend, even though, unfortunately, he is kind of a pain sometimes. He's one of those serious-type guys. You say the word "responsibility" and he snaps to attention. He's the kind of guy who always seems like he's bigger than he actually is. That's because he has that whole "I'm in charge, and you can trust me" thing going on. He has sensible brown hair, and trustworthy brown eyes, and one of those confident chins.

He also has a great sense of humor and is very smart, and I would trust him with my life any day, any time. Not that I would ever tell *him* that.

Then there's Cassie. I didn't really know her very well back then. But I think she's kind of

Jake's girlfriend now. Of course, no one is supposed to know this. *Ssshhh!* Big secret!

Cassie is the one who is least like me. If I'm comedy, she's poetry. She's a natural peacemaker. She's the one who knows when you're feeling bad and will find something nice to say that makes you feel better. And it's not like she's manipulating. She really cares about things. She's like sincere or something.

Cassie is our animal expert. Her parents are both vets and she spends most of her free time helping her dad run the Wildlife Rehabilitation Clinic. It's in the barn at their farm. They save injured woodchucks and deer and eagles and so on. Cassie actually knows how to get an injured, angry wolf to take its pills. (Not an easy thing. Believe me. I *was* a wolf once.)

You go out to her barn and you'll see this little, short, black girl in overalls and boots with her arm halfway down the throat of a wolf that could just bite it right off. And she'll be smiling and acting like it's no big deal. And the wolf will be just standing there, looking like he's trying to earn a gold star for being the best little boy in school.

Then there's Rachel. Very beautiful. Very leggy-blond-supermodel type. Ms. Fashion. Ms. Properly-Applied-Makeup. Ms. Has-It-All — Looks-*and*-Brains.

Rachel is Jake's cousin, and a total babe who, unfortunately, is also totally insane. See, somehow, underneath all that perfect hair and perfect teeth, there's this lunatic Amazon warrior-queen, just fighting to get out.

Here's what Rachel'll say whenever we decide to do something so dangerous it makes you want to wet yourself: "I'm in! Let's go! Let's do it!"

I swear that, if she could, Rachel would be wearing a suit of armor and swinging a sword. And it would be a fashionable suit of armor, and she would look great in it.

Then there is Tobias. That night in the construction site, he was just this kind of dweeby kid I barely knew. He liked Jake because Jake once kept some guys from beating him up.

To be honest with you, I don't even remember what Tobias looked like back then. Now, of course, he looks like a fierce, angry bird of prey.

There's a downside to the morphing power we have. A time limit of two hours. Stay more than two hours in a morph, and you stay forever.

That's why Tobias was flying overhead, with his wide wings catching the warm updrafts. Tobias is a hawk. A red-tail hawk, to be exact. I guess he always will be.

I tease Tobias sometimes.

What happened to him scares me.

Anyway, on that night we were cutting through

this big, abandoned construction site. It was supposed to be a shopping center, but they got it half built and then stopped.

Then, to make a long story short, there was this spaceship. It was carrying an Andalite who was dying of wounds he'd gotten fighting the Yeerks up in Earth orbit. Or thereabouts.

He's the one who told us about the Yeerks. The Yeerks are parasites. They use the bodies of other species. They take them over. They control them. That's what you call a human who's been taken over — a Controller. A human Controller.

Jake's brother, Tom, is one. A Controller.

And Melissa, Rachel's friend, her father is one, too.

The Andalites fight the Yeerks. They had been trying to stop the secret Yeerk invasion of Earth, but basically they got their butts kicked. Before he died, the Andalite promised us that reinforcements would come. Eventually. In the meantime, all he could do for us was give us a weapon.

That weapon was the power to morph. To acquire the DNA of any animal we could touch, and then to *become* that animal.

So that was the deal. The five of us, five regular everyday kids, were supposed to fight the Yeerks until the Andalites came along and rescued us.

Five kids versus the Yeerks. The Yeerks, who

had already conquered the terrifying Hork-Bajir and made them into Controllers. The Yeerks, with their creepy allies, the Taxxon-Controllers. The Yeerks who had already infiltrated human society, making Controllers out of cops and teachers and soldiers and mayors and TV newspeople. They were everywhere. They could be anyone.

And all we had was five kids who could turn into birds.

Or gorillas.

"I just don't think we should be morphing out on the street in order to get involved in everyday crimes," Jake lectured me. "Remember what happened at the used car lot with Rachel and Tobias — and you asked them if they were insane!"

I was about to argue when Rachel spoke up again.

"I think Marco did the right thing," she said. "What was he supposed to do? Just walk away? I don't think so."

"Okay, now I *know* I was wrong," I said. "Any time Rachel thinks I did the right thing, it has to be wrong. Besides, that was my whole point. I risked my life for that old man, and I don't even get a thank you."

"I don't know if it was a good idea," Cassie said, "but the feeling behind it was good. I think it was heroic."

Well, what could I say to that? It's very hard to

disagree with someone who has just called you a hero.

Jake decided to let it go. Unfortunately, the reason he decided to drop it was that he had something bigger to talk about.

He got his serious look.

I groaned. I hate that serious look. It always means trouble.

"Jake? Are you going to tell me why we're all out walking in the fields together? Aside from the fact that it's a nice day and all?"

"We're going to see Ax," Jake explained. "Cassie and I have been talking to him the last couple days. You know, about what he wants to do."

"Uh-oh," I muttered. "I just know I'm not going to like this."

"Well . . . probably not. Ax wants to go home," Jake said.

"Home?" Rachel repeated.

"To the Andalite home world," Cassie said.

Ax, whose real name is Aximili-Esgarrouth-Isthil, is an Andalite.

I stopped walking. The others stopped, too. "Um, excuse me, but isn't the Andalite home world kind of far away?"

"Ax says it's about eighty-two light years," Jake confirmed.

"Light travels about one hundred and eighty-

six thousand miles per *second*," I pointed out. "Times sixty seconds per minute. Times sixty minutes per hour. Times twenty-four hours per day. Times three hundred and sixty-five days per year. That's one light year. Times eighty-two years."

Rachel laughed. "So you *have* been staying awake in science class, Marco."

"We tried to figure it out in miles. But none of our calculators go that high," Jake said.

"You know, Jake, I could be wrong, but I don't think any of the major airlines fly to the Andalite home world," I said.

"Uh-huh," he said with a nod. "I know. That's why we'll have to steal a Yeerk spaceship."

CHAPTER 3

"There he is," Cassie said.

I followed the direction of her gaze. Over toward the line of trees at the edge of the field, I saw him.

Ax.

The Andalite.

From a distance you'd think he was a small horse or a deer. He has four hooved feet that flash with amazing speed. His upper body looks like a horse's neck and head, except that when he gets close enough, you see that he has two smaller, human-sized arms sticking out.

His head is kind of a triangle, with two huge, almond-shaped eyes. Those are his main eyes. There are two extra eyes, each stuck atop a sort

of stalk. The stalks stick out of the top of his head and move, pointing the extra eyes in any direction.

But the thing that really makes you stare is the tail.

According to Cassie and Rachel, Ax is cute. I wouldn't know, being a guy. All I know is, when you see that tail, you know right away that Andalites aren't exactly cuddly koala bears or puppies.

The Andalite tail resembles a scorpion's tail. It curls up and over, and is armed with a wicked scythe blade. They can strike with those tails faster than your eye can see.

I'd seen the first Andalite do it. In the seconds before the evil creature known as Visser Three murdered the Andalite prince, he had struck with that tail again and again.

That memory came back to me as I watched Ax galloping toward us, tail arched and ready.

"I hope there's no one around," Jake said anxiously. He scanned the area. It was pretty remote. Cassie's house and barn were way out of sight. And there was no reason why anyone would be in this distant field.

I looked up and saw Tobias's reddish tail feathers. I gave him a wave.

<All clear,> Tobias called down to us in

thought-speak. <There's some people having a picnic, but that's a couple miles from here.>

Ax came galloping up. <Prince Jake!> he said, also in thought-speak.

Jake groaned. Ax had gotten it into his head that Jake was our leader, which was partly true. And I guess for an Andalite, any leader is some kind of prince.

Ax has no mouth. No one had asked him yet how he ate with no mouth.

He communicates by thought-speech. It's the same way we communicate when we're morphed. For us humans it *only* works when we're morphed. For Andalites, it's the normal way to communicate.

"Hi, Ax," Jake said, as the Andalite came to a skidding stop just a few feet from us. "How are you doing?"

<I am well. And each of you?>

"I'm fine," Cassie said.

Tobias swooped down out of the sky. He braked and landed neatly on the grass.

"I'm fine, too, Ax," I said. "Or at least I was until I heard someone say something really stupid."

Ax looked uncertain. He swiveled one of his stalk eyes forward to get a better look at me. <What stupid thing was said?>

"Someone said we were going to try and steal a Yeerk spaceship," I said.

He smiled an Andalite smile, which is hard to describe, except that it involves his main eyes. <You think it will be dangerous?>

"Dangerous? No, jumping off a ten-story building is dangerous. Sticking your tongue in an electrical socket is dangerous — not to mention painful. But stealing a Yeerk ship is beyond dangerous."

<The higher the danger, the higher the honor,> Ax said. <Is this not true?>

I gave Rachel a sidelong look. "I think we've found your future husband."

"It may be honorable to try and get a Yeerk ship, Ax," Jake said, "but honor *isn't* our most important goal."

The Andalite looked surprised — I think. His main eyes widened, and his stalk eyes stretched up to their maximum height. It looked like surprise to me.

<What else do you fight for, if not honor?>

Jake shrugged. "Look, we're trying to do whatever we can to hurt the Yeerks. But we're also trying to stay alive. We're all there is. I mean, no one else even knows there is a Yeerk invasion. So if something happens to us . . ." He let it hang.

<I did not mean to offend,> Ax said. <You are

right, of course. You are alone. If you fail, all is lost.>

"So the question is whether this is something we can do without getting killed," Jake pointed out.

"Yeah, we're mostly against the idea of getting killed," I added. "So how are we supposed to grab a Yeerk ship? They're up in orbit. We're down here. It's not like we can call them up and ask them to come down."

<Yes, we can do that,> Ax said.

"What?"

<We can call them.>

"Right."

<I can create a Yeerk distress beacon. They will send a ship to investigate.>

"You mean like, 'Hello? Hello? Is this Visser Three? Could you send a ship down to pick me up?' " I said.

I expected everyone to laugh because the idea was so totally ridiculous. No one laughed.

"Um, excuse me?" I said, trying again. "Personally, I have had plenty of Visser Three in my life. I don't need to call him on the phone."

<It will not involve that . . . that foul beast,> Ax said.

That was one thing I liked about Ax. He hated Visser Three. He reminded me of the Andalite

prince, who was Ax's older brother. When either of them said the word "Yeerk," let alone "Visser Three," you could just feel the air vibrating from their anger.

<It will be a minor matter,> Ax said. <They will hear a distress beacon and send a Bug fighter to investigate.>

"There is always at least one Hork-Bajir and one Taxxon aboard each Bug fighter," I pointed out. "Anytime you start playing with Hork-Bajirs, it's not a minor thing."

<Do you fear them?> Ax demanded. He stared at me with all four eyes.

"You better believe I fear them."

<Fear is unworthy of a warrior.>

He seemed a little too determined for me. I don't know much about Andalites, but I had a feeling I understood this one, at least a little. See, he was alive. But every other Andalite who had come to Earth, including Ax's brother, the prince, was dead.

So I took a shot. It wasn't fair, maybe, but he'd made me mad, acting like I was some kind of coward. "How many times have you fought Hork-Bajir? Or any other Controller?" I asked him.

His stalk eyes drooped. He pawed the ground with one hoof. <Never,> he said.

I nodded. "I thought so. So let me tell you

something, Ax. It's scary. It's so scary that sometimes you wish you could just go ahead and die because it's easier than dealing with the terror."

Well, I thought as I looked around at my friends, *that pretty well killed everyone's happy mood.*

It was Tobias who broke the silence. <If you get a Yeerk ship, can you get back to the Andalite home world?>

Ax seemed abashed, but he answered, <Yes. I hope so.>

<And if you make it, can you do anything to hurry your people up? To get them back here quicker?>

<I am young. Like you. But I am the brother of Prince Elfangor. My people will listen to me. I . . . I know that they will come, either way. But yes, perhaps if I can return and tell them how desperate your situation is . . .>

Jake took a deep breath. "Okay. Time for a vote."

I groaned. I already knew what it would be.

CHAPTER 4

"Okay, ready?" I asked.

<Yes. I am prepared to begin the morph,> Ax said.

It was Saturday. A couple of days after we had all agreed to go ahead with the plan to capture a Yeerk ship. We were in Cassie's barn, surrounded by cages full of injured animals and birds. Cassie's father and mother were both away for the day.

Jake checked his watch. "Ten after ten," he reported.

"Ax starts morphing at ten-twelve and is done by ten-fifteen. The bus will be at the stop at ten twenty-five," I said. "It will arrive at the mall at eleven. By that point Ax will have been in morph for forty-five minutes. That leaves an hour and fifteen minutes on the two-hour morph time."

"Is it enough time?" Cassie wondered. She was biting her lip nervously.

I shrugged. "Thirty minutes to reach Radio Shack, find what Ax needs to make his transmitter, buy it and get back to catch the eleven-thirty bus home. That gets back here at five after twelve. Ten minutes to spare."

Jake was looking pretty stony-faced, which is how he looks when he's not sure if something will work.

"It's the best we can do," I said.

"I know. Everyone ready?" Jake asked.

"I should go *with* you guys," Rachel said for like the tenth time that morning. "I should be there."

"No. We can't *all* go. If something goes wrong, we don't want everyone caught at once," I said. "And something is sure to go wrong."

<Why do you say that?!> Ax demanded sharply.

Jake smiled. "Marco doesn't believe in optimism."

Tobias flew almost silently into the barn through the open hayloft. <It's still all clear. And the bus is right on schedule, over on Margolis Avenue.>

"Okay, Ax. Time to morph," Jake said.

"And, um, don't forget the morphing outfit, okay?" I reminded him. The concept of clothing kind of puzzled the Andalite. We'd gotten him skintight bike shorts and a T-shirt that he could use for morphing, but he still didn't know why.

It's one of the most annoying things about morphing — dealing with clothing. We'd learned how to morph clothing, but only things that were real tight-fitting. Any time you tried to morph a jacket or sweater they just ended up shredded. And shoes? Forget about shoes.

<Clothing, yes,> he said. <I have integrated it into my human morph.>

"Time," Jake said, pointing at his watch.

Ax began to change.

I'd only seen him do it once before — soon after we rescued him from the sunken Andalite dome ship.

I've seen a lot of morphing. I've done a lot of it, too. It's always creepy watching a human being become some strange animal. But watching Ax morph was different. He wasn't becoming an animal. He was becoming a human being.

The stalk eyes shrank and disappeared in his head. The deadly scorpion tail shriveled and withered and slithered up inside him like someone sucking up a piece of spaghetti.

His front hooves disappeared completely.

"Whoa, look out," Jake said. He caught the Andalite as he fell forward, with no front legs to support him.

<Thank you. I must practice standing with only two legs.>

A gash opened in his face and grew lips and teeth. A nose grew where there had just been small vertical slits. His eyes became smaller, more human.

But the weirdest thing about Ax morphing was not just that he looked like a human. It was that he looked like a *particular* human.

Actually, *four* particular humans. See, he had absorbed DNA from Jake and Cassie and Rachel and me. Somehow, by some process we did not understand, he was able to combine all four genetic patterns to come up with one person.

The end result was definitely strange and disturbing.

I looked at him and saw some of myself, and Jake, and Rachel and Cassie, too, although Ax was male. That was the most bizarre part. Looking at him and thinking, *Hey, he looks familiar. Really familiar. In fact, hey, that's* my *hair!*

"Ax, you could be either a really pretty guy, or a kind of unattractive girl," I said.

"I am an Andalite," he said. "Andalite. Lite. Ite."

"Okay, put on those additional clothes," Jake said. "Let's get going. Tobias?" He looked up to the rafters.

<On my way. I'll check on the bus,> Tobias said, and flew away.

"More clothing? Clo. Clo-theeeeng. Clo-theeng?" Ax said.

"Ax? Don't do that," I said.

"What? Wha wha wha. Tuh."

"That. Where you play with the sounds. Just say what you need to say, and stop."

Like I said, the Andalites have no mouths and no spoken speech. Ax seemed to think mouths were some kind of toy.

"Yes," Ax agreed. "Yah. Ess."

"And one other thing? The shoes go on your feet. Not in your pockets."

"Yes. I remember. Mem. Ber." He pulled his sneakers out of his pockets and looked at them helplessly. Rachel and Cassie each took a foot and got him laced up.

"People are going to think he's weird," Rachel said, sounding exasperated.

"Fortunately, it's the mall on a Saturday morning," I pointed out. "It'll be full of weird people."

"Not *this* weird," Rachel said. "This could be trouble."

"Isn't it a little late for you to admit that I was

right and this idea is insane?" I asked her. "Besides, no need to worry. I'll be there."

"Great. Then it's sure to be a disaster."

We caught the bus without any problem. Ax made strange mouth noises the entire trip, but the bus was mostly empty.

We got to the mall right on time.

"So far, so good," Jake said as we headed into the mall.

I rolled my eyes. "Jake? Do me a favor. Don't ever say 'so far, so good.' The only time anyone *ever* says 'so far, so good' is right before everything blows up in his face."

"So far. So far. Farrrrr. Faaaar," Ax said, trying out the sounds. "So. Sssso far so so so good."

"Oh, man," I said.

CHAPTER 5

The mall was a zoo. Wall-to-wall people. Old people moving real slow. Married people with squalling babies in big huge strollers. High school kids trying to look cool. Mall police trying to look tough. Good-looking girls carrying bags from The Limited.

Your basic Saturday at the mall.

"Okay, where is Radio Shack?" Jake wondered.

"I don't know," I said.

"Is it up on the second level? You know, down by Sears?"

"Is that it? Or is that Circuit City?"

"Let me check the map over there. Ax? Come on with . . ." Jake stopped suddenly. "Marco? Where is Ax?"

I spun around. "He was right here!"

Bodies everywhere! All I saw were bodies. Men, women, boys, girls, babies. But no aliens. At least not that I could see. We had lost Ax!

It had taken a total of about two minutes for us to mess up.

Then, suddenly, I saw a strangely familiar face.

"There he is! On the escalator!"

"How did he get all the way over there?" Jake demanded.

We took off after him, but it was so crowded we could barely move. Jake started pushing his way through. I grabbed him by the arm.

"Don't run, man. The mall cops will think you're ripping something off. Besides, we can't attract attention. Controllers shop, too."

Jake slowed instantly. "You're right. This many people, some of them are sure to be Controllers."

We threaded our way, moving as quickly as we could without being too obvious. I just kept saying "excuse me, excuse me," and tried not to bump into anyone who looked like he'd get mad and pound me.

It seemed to take forever to reach the escalator. By then we had totally lost sight of Ax.

"As long as he doesn't demorph we're okay," Jake said. "I mean, what's the worst he could do?"

"Jake, I don't want to think about the worst he could do," I said.

"There!"

"Where?"

"Over at Starbucks. The coffee place."

I'm not as tall as Jake so I couldn't see him as easily. But as we got near Starbucks, I spotted him. He was standing patiently in line.

We got to him just in time to hear him say, "I'll have . . . I-yull, Ile, have a double latte, too. Double. Bull. Bull. Latay ay ay."

"He must have heard someone else say it," I whispered to Jake.

"Caff or decaf?" the clerk asked.

Ax stared. "Caff? Caff caff caff?"

"That will be two ninety-five."

Ax stared some more. "Fi-ive."

Jake reached into his pocket and yanked out the money he'd brought to pay for things at Radio Shack. "Here you go," he said, peeling off three dollars.

I took Ax's arm and guided him to the pickup window. "Ax, *don't* go off on your own, okay? We almost lost you."

"Lost? I am here. Hee-yar."

"Yeah, look, just stay close, okay?" I gave Jake a look. "See? It's your fault. You said, 'so far, so good.'"

The Starbucks guy handed Ax a paper cup.

Ax took it. He looked around to see what other people were doing. Like them, he put a lid on his cup.

Then, still mimicking the others, he attempted to drink.

"Um, Ax?" I said. "You have to drink where the little hole is in the lid."

"A hole! In the lid! No spills! Ills!"

This was the coolest thing Ax had ever seen. I guess coffee cup technology hasn't advanced very far on the Andalite home world. Probably because they don't have mouths, and so drinking is not a big concern. But whatever the reason, Ax wouldn't shut up about it.

"So simple! Imple. And yet so effective!"

"Yeah, it's a real miracle of human technology," I said.

"I have wanted to try other mouth uses. Drinking. Eating." Then, as an afterthought, he added, "Eeee-ting. Ting."

"Just line the little hole up with your mouth," I said. "Come on, there's Radio Shack. We've already lost like ten minutes."

The two of us hemmed Ax in and herded him toward Radio Shack.

Then he drank the coffee.

"Ahhh! Ohhh! Oh, oh, oh, what? What? What is that?!"

"What?" I asked, alarmed. I swiveled my head back and forth, looking for some danger.

"A new sense. It . . . I cannot explain it. It is . . . it comes from this mouth." He pointed at his mouth. "It happened when I drank this liquid. It was pleasant. Very pleasant."

It took a few seconds for Jake and I to realize what he was talking about. "Oh. Taste! He's tasting it," Jake said. "He doesn't normally have the sense of taste."

"At least he stopped repeating sounds," I muttered.

"Taste," Ax said, contradicting me. "Aste. Tuh-aste."

He drank his coffee and we rushed him to Radio Shack. "Okay, look, Ax, we have very little time. See if the stuff you need is here."

I'll say this for Ax. He may have been a little weird by human standards, but the boy knows his technology. I mean, he went down the pegboards in the back of the store and just started lifting off different components.

"This must be a primitive *gairtmof,*" he said, inspecting a small switch. "And this could be a sort of *fleer.* Very primitive, but it will work."

In ten minutes' time he'd accumulated a dozen components, ranging from coaxial cable to batteries to things I didn't even recognize.

"Good," he said at last. "All I lack is a Z-Space transponder. Transponder. PONder."

"A what?"

"A Z-Space transponder. It translates the signal into zero space."

I looked at Jake. "Zero space?"

Jake looked back at me and shrugged. "Never heard of it."

Ax looked doubtful. "Zero space," he repeated. "Zeeeero. The opposite of true space. Anti-reality." He looked patiently from one of us to the other. "Zero space, the nondimension where faster-than-light travel is possible. Bull. Possi-bull-uh."

"Oh," I said sarcastically. "*That* zero space. Um, Ax? Sorry to be so primitive and all, but we don't have faster-than-light travel. And I've never heard of zero space."

"Oh."

"Yeah. *Oh.*"

"Let's get this stuff and worry about the other thing later," Jake said calmly. But I could tell he was getting slightly hacked off. "I'll go pay for this stuff."

Ax drained the last of his coffee. "Taste," he said. "I would like more taste." He cocked his head. "I smell things. I believe . . . buh-leeve . . . blee . . . bleeve . . . there is a connection between smell and taste."

"Yeah, you're right," I said. "We can't travel faster than light, but we can make a sticky bun that smells pretty good."

"Sticky," Ax said. "Must I carry this?" he asked, indicating his empty coffee cup.

"No, you can just throw it away."

Bad choice of words. Ax threw the coffee cup. He threw it hard. It hit one of the cashiers in the head.

"Hey!"

"Sorry, it was an accident, man," I yelped, rushing to the cashier. "He's . . . he's sick. He, um, has this condition. You know, like out-of-control spasms."

Jake said, "Yeah, it's not his fault. It's like a seizure!"

The clerk rubbed his head. "Okay, forget it. Besides, he's out of here and that's all I care about."

"He's what?"

Jake and I turned fast. But Ax was gone.

Jake grabbed the bag of stuff and raced after me out into the stream of people.

Ax was nowhere to be seen.

But then I looked down at the lower level. There was a crowd of people kind of surging. All moving in the same direction. Like they were running to see something.

"They're heading toward the food court," Jake said.

"Oh, I have a *very* bad feeling about this," I said.

We ran for the escalator. We shoved down it, yelling "excuse me" every two seconds.

We got to the food court. We wormed our way through a crowd of laughing, giggling, pointing people.

And there, all alone — because all the sane people had pulled away — was Ax.

He was racing like some lunatic from table to table, snatching up leftover food and shoving it in his mouth.

As I watched he grabbed a half-eaten slice of pizza.

"Taste!" he yelled as he scarfed a huge bite. He threw the rest of the pizza through the air. It just missed the mall cop who was closing in on him.

Ax couldn't care less. He had found a piece of Cinnabun. "This was the smell!" he cried. He jammed the roll in his mouth. "Ahhh! Ahhh! Taste! Taste! Wonderful! Ful. Ful."

"They *do* make a good sticky bun," I muttered to Jake.

"We have to get him out of here," Jake hissed.

"Too late. Look! Three more mall cops."

The cops jumped at Ax.

Ax decided it was a good time to throw the rest of the bun away. It hit the nearest cop in the face.

"Ax! Run! Run!" I yelled.

I guess I got through, because Ax ran.

Unfortunately, he couldn't run very well in his two-legged human morph.

So as he ran and stumbled, chased by huffing, puffing mall police, he began to change.

CHAPTER 6

"Stop!" a cop yelled. "I am ordering you to halt!"

But Ax wasn't interested in halting. He was panicked.

A woman stepped out of the Body Shop holding a bag full of colorful jars. Ax plowed into her. The bag went flying.

The stalks began to grow out of the top of his head. The extra eyes appeared on the ends and turned backward to watch the people chasing him.

Jake and I were two of those people. We were ahead of the cops, but not by much. Fortunately, I guess the cops assumed we were just idiots running along for fun.

I could hear one of the cops yelling into his walkie-talkie. "Cut him off at the east entrance!"

Legs began to grow from the chest of Ax's human morph. His own front legs, small at first, but growing rapidly.

He was slowing down as his human legs began to change. The knees were reversing direction. His spine elongated into the beginnings of a tail.

That's when the screaming started.

"Ahhh ahhhhh!"

"What is it? What IS it?"

People were screaming and running and dropping their bags as they caught a glimpse of the nightmare creature Ax had become. Half-human, half-Andalite. A fluid, shifting mess of half-formed features.

I couldn't blame them. I felt like screaming myself.

We were getting near the exit, racing past the shoe repair place.

Suddenly, Ax fell forward, tangled up in his own mutating legs. He skidded down the polished marble floor.

Most of the crowd had been left behind, but the mall police were still with us.

"You kids get out of the way!" one of them yelled at us. "This guy could be dangerous."

Ax sprang up. He was much more sure of himself, now that he was on his four Andalite hooves. The morph was almost entirely complete. His mouth was gone. His extra eyes were in place. His two arms and four legs were fully formed.

Then, at the very last, the tail appeared.

It was then that I heard the nearest mall cop, in an awed, frightened whisper, say, “Andalite!”

I quickly turned and looked at him. Only a Controller would recognize an Andalite.

The Controller cop drew his gun from his holster.

“RUN!” I yelled at Ax.

The Controller stood between Ax and the door. Big mistake. The Andalite tail flashed, faster than my eyes could follow. The cop’s gun went flying through the air. He clutched at a hand that was red with blood.

Out the door we blew, running for our lives.

Sirens!

“Those are real cops coming,” I said. “Not mall rent-a-cops!”

<Where should we go?> Ax demanded, reverting to thought-speak.

“Oh, *now* he wants advice?!” I looked around frantically. The bus was not going to be an option. The mall cops poured from the glass doors. The city police screamed toward us in their black-and-whites.

All we could do was run. So we ran. Up rows

of parked cars. Two kids and a guy who did not belong on this planet.

"The grocery store!" Jake yelled.

"What?" I gasped. I was getting tired.

"In there!" he pointed. It was the grocery store across the parking lot. It was the only way we could go.

Police cars screeched to a halt all around us.

"Freeze!"

"I don't think so," I said.

We jetted through the big glass doors of the supermarket at a full, panicked run. I halfway expected to hear guns firing and bullets whizzing.

"Jake!" I yelled. "Help me here!" I had an idea for slowing down our pursuers. I grabbed a big row of parked grocery carts and shoved them back toward the doors. Jake grabbed on and helped.

Then we were off and running again, with Ax skittering shakily on the slippery floor and banging into groceries. Cans of olives and tomatoes crashed behind him.

Customers screamed and crashed their carts into each other.

"It's a monster! Mommy, it's a monster!" some little kid yelled.

"It's just a pretend monster," his mother said.

Yeah. A pretend monster. Right.

Then I saw our way out. It was at the end of

the aisle. But I needed some time. I needed to get everyone out of our way. We couldn't have witnesses.

"There's a bomb!" I screamed, at the top of my lungs. "BOMB!"

"What?" Jake demanded.

"There's a bomb! A bomb in the store! Run! Run! Everyone out! A BOMB!"

"What are you doing?!" Jake yelled.

"The cops have the place surrounded. There's only one way out," I snapped. I pointed.

I pointed at the live lobster tank at the end of the aisle by the seafood counter.

"Oh, no," Jake groaned.

"Oh, yes." I grinned.

The shoppers were running in panic, either from the supposed bomb or just from Ax. But the baskets in the doorway and the people shoving to escape slowed the cops down for a precious few moments.

I had a feeling the Controller cops were making sure that no real cops came in after us. They wanted us for themselves. With no human witnesses.

"Let's go for a swim," I said.

It was a big lobster tank, fortunately. I hoisted myself up the side and climbed in. Jake was right behind me. We each grabbed a lobster and threw one to Ax.

It was not easy "acquiring" the lobster. It took concentration. And all I could think was that there were an awful lot of cops outside the store, probably getting ready to rush in. And they would all have guns.

The lobster went limp and passive, the way animals do when you acquire them.

I dropped him back in the water. We stripped off our outer clothes and shoes and stuffed them, along with the Radio Shack bag, in a trash can.

Ax had already begun to morph. Jake and I waited till he had shrunk a little and then hauled him into the tank with us.

He was already hard, like armor, and his arms had begun to split open and swell.

Then I began the morph.

I've been afraid a lot since we became Animorphs. But I have not gotten used to it. And I can tell you, I was so scared my bones were rattling.

At any second they were going to rush in.

At any moment they were going to catch us half-morphed.

I looked over at Jake. His eyes were gone, replaced by little black BBs.

"Ewww."

As I watched, eight spindly, blue, insectlike legs erupted from his chest.

"Aaaaahhh!" I yelped in shock.

Jake's face seemed to open up, to split open into a complex mess of valves. I think I would have thrown up, seeing that. Except that I, also, no longer had a mouth.

At that very moment, I felt antennae explode from my forehead like impossibly long spears.

I was shrinking as I morphed, falling, falling, falling down into the water which had been around my thighs and was now around my neck.

I had the terrifying sensation of knowing that all the bones inside my body were dissolving, as a hard, fingernail-like crust covered me all over.

My human body was melting away.

My human vision was fading. I could no longer see the way a human sees.

Which was a good thing. Because I really did not want to see what I was becoming.

CHAPTER 7

I think I might have just started screaming and never stopped. But I no longer had a mouth, or throat, or vocal cords capable of making sounds.

I had four sets of legs. I had two huge pincers. I could see them, kind of. They were a fractured image in my lobster eyes. I couldn't see much of the rest of me. But I could see other lobsters in the water.

I was very frightened.

Eat.

Eat.

Kill and eat.

The lobster brain surfaced suddenly, bubbling

up within my human awareness. It had two thoughts.

Eat.

Eat.

Kill and eat.

I was getting input from senses I couldn't begin to understand. My extraordinarily long antennae felt water temperature, and water current, and vibration. But I didn't know what any of it meant.

My eyes were almost useless at first. They showed fractured, incredible images, with none of the colors I knew.

I could see my pincers out in front of me. I could see my antennae. And behind me I could see a curved, brownish-blue surface, with humps and bumps on it.

My body! I realized with a sickening sensation. That was my back. My hard shell.

I could not look down and see my belly, or the hairy swimmerets scurrying away, back beneath my tail. I could not see my eight spiderlike legs, but I could feel as they propelled me suddenly, scrabbling along the glass bottom of the tank.

<Jake?> I called out.

<Yeah. I'm here,> he said. He sounded shaky. Which was fine, because I was on the verge of crying. If lobsters could cry.

<You okay?>

<Yeah. This is not my favorite morph, though.>

<No,> I agreed. It was good being able to talk to him. I mean, you'd think you were losing your mind otherwise.

<Ax?> Jake called.

<I . . . I feel. . . . I am hungry. This animal wants to eat,> Ax answered.

<Yeah, well, that's pretty normal for morphs,> I said. <Most animals care about food and not much else. I don't think lobsters are exactly geniuses.>

<It wants to find prey,> Ax said wonderingly.

<I know. Who'd have figured lobsters were predators?> I said.

<It's easier to deal with a predator brain than with prey. That prey fear can be overwhelming,> Jake said.

I saw a lobster close by. <Is that you, Jake? Wiggle your left pincer.>

The left pincer did not move. I realized this lobster had a rubber band around his pincer. None of us had rubber bands. Rubber bands were not a part of the lobster DNA.

I saw a lobster to my left, unbanded. And another behind him. That was the three of us. There were half a dozen rubber-banded lobsters floating or just sitting.

<Speaking of fear,> I said. <Can anyone see out of the tank?>

<Just shadows,> Jake said. <These are pathetic eyes.>

<Yes, even worse than your human eyes,> Ax commented.

<This is really creepy,> I said. <I've never had an exoskeleton before.>

<These pincers are most excellent, though,> Ax said.

I saw him opening and closing them.

<Ax?> Jake said. <You say you can keep track of time accurately? Start tracking.>

<Yes, Prince Jake,> Ax said. <So far, ten of your minutes have passed.>

<That much?> I was surprised. <Ten minutes? The cops must have come in by now.>

<I was thinking the same thing,> Jake said.

<We better wait as long as we can. Close to the full two hours,> I said. <Although I really don't want to spend any more time than I have to in this creepy morph.>

According to Ax, an hour had passed when it happened.

I felt a strange disturbance in the water. Something large had splashed in. I sensed something above me.

Before I could think or react, I felt pressure on my shell.

I was rising rapidly through the water, being lifted.

<Jake! Something has me!>

Sudden shock!

I was out of the water.

Dryness. Heat. My antennae waved wildly as I tried to understand. My eyes registered nothing but bright light and huge, indistinct shadows.

Something large closed my right pincer forcibly. I could not open it. Then my left.

Rubber bands! I couldn't see them in this waterless environment. I was nearly blind. But I knew what had happened.

Someone had picked me up and rubberbanded my pincers.

Then I was tumbling, sliding, rubbing against things I could tell were other lobsters.

<Jake! Are you in this, too?>

<Yeah, but don't ask me what it means. I can't see or hear very well.>

<Is it them? Is it Controllers?>

Something very cold dropped on me and slithered around my body.

Ice?

I felt a sensation of swinging back and forth for a while, like being on a swing.

<Ax?>

<Yes, Marco. I am here, too. What is happening?>

<You got me,> I said. <Maybe the cops

have us. Maybe the Controllers have us. I don't know.>

<Let's stay in morph as long as we can,> Jake said. <Maybe we'll figure it out. But if the Controllers have us, the last thing we want to do is demorph.>

The ice seemed to be making me sleepy. Or not exactly sleepy, just slow. Sluggish.

I guess I kind of zoned out for a while. I didn't know for how long, until I became suddenly alert and heard Ax's drowsy voice in my head saying, <We have only seven minutes left.>

That jolted me. I was not about to spend the rest of my life trapped as a lobster.

<Okay, I am *out* of this morph, I don't care who sees,> I yelled.

<Agreed,> Jake said. <Time's up. We have to take our chances.>

<At least it's warmer now,> I said. I tried to look around, but my antennae felt nothing in the air. And my eyes only saw meaningless, blurry gray forms.

I focused on demorphing. I wondered if I could close my human eyes when Jake started to reappear. I really did not want to watch Jake and Ax demorph. Once had been enough. I would already have nightmares for a month.

<Here goes,> I said. I began the change.

But just then I again felt the sensation of pressure on my shell. My pincers came free. Someone, or something, had removed the rubber bands.

And suddenly I felt a warmth billowing up around me.

Steam.

<Oh, no.>

CHAPTER 8

<NOOOOOO!> I screamed silently.

I knew where I was! I was in someone's hand, about to be dropped into a pot of boiling water.

<NOOOOOOOOO!>

And maybe it was because I was so desperate to scream, or maybe it was just the luck of the morph, but my human mouth was one of the first things to emerge.

Small, open lips appeared in place of my lobster mouth.

I didn't have normal lungs or vocal cords yet, so I couldn't make a sound.

But I guess I didn't have to.

I guess suddenly having lips appear on a lobster was enough to make the woman drop me.

I fell. My front pincers caught the edge of the pan. Sheer dumb luck. I hung onto the edge of the pan as my tail curled up, inches above the boiling water in the pot.

I grew rapidly, becoming a baby-sized creature half-covered with hard cuticle, half flesh. Human eyes grew in place of the useless stalk eyes. The antennae sucked back into my forehead. I heard a grinding sound as my spine reappeared inside me.

With a desperate surge of energy, I tumbled over the side of the pan and landed flat on my shell back, atop the stove. I was looking up into a stove hood.

I rolled away from the heat and fell.

But the fall wasn't far, because I was now the size of a toddler, more human than lobster. I was one nasty-looking kid, though, with eight legs growing from my stomach and chest.

My human hearing returned with shocking effect.

"Ahhhhhh! Ahhhhhhh! Ahhhhhh! Ahhhhhhh! Ahhhhhhh!"

Someone was screaming uncontrollably.

My legs were back! I stood up. I looked around and saw a woman. Sort of pretty, except for the fact that her eyes were wide with terror and she was screaming.

"Ahhhhhhhh! Ahhhhhhhhh! Ahhhhhhhh!"

I glanced over and saw the plastic bag filled with ice. That's how she had carried us from the supermarket. Now we were in her kitchen. Jake was already mostly human, standing with one foot still in the grocery bag. The eight legs sucked into his chest. His human eyes appeared.

Ax was a truly disgusting combination of Andalite and lobster. But as I watched, he eliminated the last traces of crustacean.

Unfortunately, this did not make the woman feel any better.

"Ahhhhhhhhh! Ahhhhhhhhhh! Ahhhhhhhh!"

"It's okay, ma'am," I said. "We're not going to hurt you."

"Calm down, ma'am," Jake said. "Please calm down."

Her eyes darted wildly from me to Jake to Ax. She kept screaming.

"Ahhhhhhhhh! Ahhhhhhhhh! Ahhhhhhh!"

"Look, it's okay," I said. "We're going to leave. No one is going to hurt you."

"You . . . you . . . you . . . you . . . lobsters!" she managed to say.

"Yeah, it is slightly weird, I'll admit," I said. "But it's okay. It's just a dream."

"A . . . a . . . a dream?"

"Yes, ma'am. Just a dream," Jake said reassuringly.

I looked at Ax. "Can you morph to human yet? We need to get out of here."

"I can morph again," he assured me. And he started right away.

"We're going to leave now," Jake said. "You can wake up later, okay? But I wouldn't tell anyone about this dream."

The woman shook her head violently.

"See, it could get you in trouble with . . . with certain people. Besides, folks would just think you're crazy."

She nodded with extreme conviction.

Ax was almost human. We were all dressed in our slightly ridiculous morphing outfits, but they would have to do.

We headed for the door. Then I caught sight of three more lobsters, still in the bag of ice. I guess it was supposed to be a dinner for six.

"Ma'am?" I asked. "Do us a favor, would you, please? Take those other guys down to the beach and let them go. Okay?"

CHAPTER 9

Jake and I were playing video games at the mall. I was kicking his butt. He was distracted because he was eating.

He was eating a big red bug with huge pincers.

I told him not to eat it. It would upset his stomach. But he just ignored me.

Then, suddenly, his stomach exploded. It just exploded outward, guts flying everywhere. Eight huge spider legs appeared, like something in him was trying to crawl out.

I tried to get away, but the steam was rising. I was burning up!

I tried to run, but my legs were gone, replaced by a tail that jerked and kicked.

I screamed.

And screamed.

"Marco, Marco, wake up!"

My eyes opened very suddenly. Darkness. Someone holding onto me. I was confused.

"Mom?" I asked.

Silence. Then, "No."

My brain snapped back into reality. I was in my room. In my own bed. My dad was sitting on the side of the bed. He looked concerned and sad.

"It's just me," he said. He let go of my shoulders.

I felt sweaty all over. Cold sweat.

"I guess you had a nightmare," my father said.

"Yeah," I said shakily. "Sorry I woke you up."

"I wasn't asleep," he said.

I glanced at my clock. The red numbers showed 3:18 A.M. I didn't have to ask why my dad was awake. He often sat awake late into the night. Sometimes watching TV. Sometimes just staring into space.

He'd been that way since my mom died.

My dad looks very different from me. For one thing, he's pretty tall. He's paler than me, too, and has light brown eyes. My mom was Hispanic, very dark hair and eyes. Everyone says I look like her. I know it's true, because sometimes when he's thinking about her, my dad will just glaze over and stare at me like I'm not even there. Like I'm a picture of someone else.

"I'm okay now," I said. "You should try to get some sleep."

He nodded. "Yeah. I'll do that. Look, Marco, you weren't dreaming about *her,* were you?"

"No, Dad. Why?"

"Because the first thing you said when you woke up was 'Mom.' "

"I guess I was confused."

"Do you ever? Dream about her, I mean?"

"Sometimes," I admitted. "But they aren't nightmares."

He almost smiled. "No. I guess they wouldn't be, would they?" He picked up the little framed picture of my mom that I keep on my nightstand. Then he got that twisted look of sick grief I had seen on his face every day for the last two years.

Part of me is mad when I see him that way. Part of me just wants to say, "Dad, get it together. Let her go. She's dead. She doesn't want us spending the rest of our lives mourning."

But I never do say that.

After a few minutes, he got up. He made some last remark about how I shouldn't be worried about bogeymen, and left. I knew he would sit out in the living room alone, and eventually fall asleep in his chair.

I lay there in the dark and tried to get the dream out of my head. But it's hard to forget a nightmare that's true.

<There. It is finished.> Ax held up a small mess of electronic components for all of us to see. It looked sort of like an exploded remote control, but smaller.

It was the next day. We were out in the woods, grouped together beneath a huge old oak tree. It was like a strange sort of picnic. Jake and Cassie had each brought hand tools for Ax to use — screwdrivers, a solder gun, a battery-powered drill, a hammer, wrenches, pliers and, of course we had the electronic parts we had stashed in the trash before the lobster incident.

Rachel had brought sandwiches. I'd brought a six-pack of Pepsi.

It was a nice day, sunny and warm. I needed a nice day. I needed sunlight. I'd had a bad night, with too little sleep.

"So, Ax," I said. "What is it?"

<It is a distress beacon that can broadcast on Yeerk frequencies,> he said with satisfaction. <I know this is a Yeerk frequency. We have used it to trick them before. To send false instructions.>

"All it needs is a Z-Space transponder," Jake said wearily, rolling his eyes at me.

I think Jake may have been a bit ragged out

by the lobster incident, too. He seemed snappish and kind of unfocused. Not at all Jake-like.

"And since we can't get a Z-Space transponder, it's basically useless, right?" Rachel asked.

<Yes. Totally useless without the transponder.>

Rachel threw up her hands. "Then what exactly are we doing?"

Jake just shrugged. Cassie sidled up next to him and gave him a small little sideways hug. No one was supposed to notice. But right away Jake's harsh look mellowed a little.

That wasn't doing anything for *my* bad mood, though. "Well, I'm guessing that in about two centuries or so, humans will discover zero space and make transponders. Whatever *they* are. But in the meantime, I'm going to have a sandwich."

Tobias came drifting down through the branches and leaves of the tree, almost silent. He landed on a low branch of the oak. <No one anywhere near here,> he reported. <Looks safe. At least as far as you guys are concerned. But there's a golden eagle about a quarter-mile south. I think I'll stay out of sight for a while and hope he goes away.>

Not for the first time, I realized how tough Tobias's life is. He shares all the same dangers we do, but he also has all the dangers that come from being a red-tail hawk. Golden eagles some-

times prey on hawks. They are bigger and faster than he is.

<So. What's up?> Tobias asked.

"We have a completely useless distress beacon," Rachel said. "We need a transponder that probably won't be invented on this planet for a century or two."

<How about Chapman?> Tobias said.

"What about Chapman?" I asked. Chapman is the assistant principal at our school. He's also one of the most important Controllers.

I used to hate Chapman. I mean, once I knew that he was a Controller and all. But then we learned that he surrendered his freedom to the Yeerks as part of a deal to keep his daughter, Melissa, safe.

It's hard to hate someone for protecting their kid. Even if he or she ended up being a deadly enemy. That's one of the terrible things about fighting the Yeerks. The real enemy is just the evil slug in a person's brain. The host is often totally innocent.

<We know that Chapman communicates with Visser Three,> Tobias said. <He talks to Visser Three on the Yeerk mother ship, or on the Blade ship. Wherever Visser Three is. Doesn't that mean that Chapman's secret radio thing must have one of these Z-Space transponders?>

<Yes!> Ax said instantly. <If this Controller

speaks to any Yeerk ship, he would have to have a Z-Space transponder. The Yeerk ships are all cloaked. Cloaking technology requires a Z-Space deflection.>

Jake caught my eye. "That's pretty much what I figured."

I smiled, despite the fact that I had a bad feeling about the way this conversation was going.

"How big is a Z-Space thingie?" Cassie asked.

Ax held two of his fingers close together, indicating something the size of a pea. <There would be several redundant units in any transmitter. We could take one without it being noticed. At least not right away.>

Rachel stood. "We are not going into Chapman's house again," she said firmly. "The last time we did, we almost got Melissa made into a Controller. We cannot morph her cat again. Chapman is on guard now. It won't be easy this time." She realized what she'd said and added, "Not that it was exactly easy the first time."

"A historic first," I observed. "Rachel saying 'no' to a mission."

"Rachel's right," Jake said. "We do *nothing* that will endanger Melissa again. So the cat is out. Also any other plan that means major risk that Chapman will discover us."

For a while no one said anything.

Finally Ax spoke silently in our heads. <I cannot ask anyone to take risks for me. You rescued me from the bottom of the ocean. You sheltered me. And my foolishness almost got Prince Jake and Marco killed yesterday.>

What he said surprised me a little. I guess I'd expected him to argue that we should try and help him.

"What if . . ." Cassie began.

We all looked at her. "Yes?" Jake asked.

"What if there was a way to get into Chapman's basement room — the secret room where he keeps the transmitter — without even going through the house? With almost no chance of getting caught?"

I felt my heart sink. "As long as it doesn't involve anything with an exoskeleton."

I'd meant it as a joke. But Cassie just looked at me solemnly.

"What?" I demanded. "A lobster again? How is a lobster —"

"No," she said. "Think smaller. Much smaller. Much, much smaller."

CHAPTER 10

Ants. That was Cassie's brilliant idea. Ants.

See, ants could get into Chapman's basement. And ants could carry away the small transponder.

Ants.

This was what my life had come to. We ended up spending a couple of hours debating whether we should be red ants or black ants. I finally left in disgust. I didn't want to be an ant, red, black, or any other color.

I saw Jake the next day in school. I had just come out of history class, where I had blown a pop quiz.

I wasn't in the best mood.

I was opening my locker and muttering about

the Mexican-American War, and how was anyone supposed to remember the difference between that war and the Texas war of independence.

"Hi," Jake said. "The answer is black. Turns out most of the ants near Chapman's house are black. Tobias checked it out."

I looked over Jake's shoulder to make sure no one was close enough to overhear. "Jake, I don't want to be a bug. I've been a gorilla, an osprey, a dolphin, a seagull, a trout, of all things, a lobster . . . and I'm probably forgetting a few. Gorilla was fun. Dolphin was fun. Osprey was fun. Ant? Not fun. Basically, bugs are a bad idea."

Jake shrugged. "I was a flea. That was no big thing." He grinned like he'd made the world's funniest joke. "Seriously, it was like nothing. I couldn't see anything. I could barely hear anything, just vibrations. All I knew was I liked warm bodies and whenever I got hungry I just poked a hole in some warm skin."

"And sucked blood."

He looked a little uncomfortable. "Well, it was Rachel's blood. Kind of. I mean, okay, it was cat blood, but Rachel was morphing the cat."

"Jake? Do you ever listen to yourself?"

"I try not to think about it," he admitted. "But look, we want to try and give Ax a chance to get home. And if he stays here he's a danger to us. We've got this big Anda —" He looked around to make sure no one could hear, and lowered his voice. "We have this big Andalite running around Cassie's farm. What if someone sees him? Any Controller is going to know what he is. And they're going to wonder why he's on Cassie's land."

I nodded. "Yeah. You're right. But I almost died the other day. I was almost boiled alive. I know you're the big hero type, Jake, but I'm not."

I grabbed my book out of the locker, slammed the door, and headed down the hall. Jake kept pace.

"You know what next Sunday is?" I asked him suddenly. I hadn't planned to say anything.

"Sunday? I don't know. What?"

"Two years, to the day. Two years since my mom died. And I don't know what to do. I don't know whether I should talk to my dad about it, or just let it pass. But I know one thing — this would be a really bad week for me to turn up dead."

I kept walking. He didn't follow me.

Two years.

She'd taken the boat out of the marina. She'd sailed it out into a rough sea. No one knew why. She'd never done it before. We'd always gone out together, the three of us.

That night, after the high winds had blown past, they found the boat driven up onto the

rocks. The hull was shattered. There was no sign of my mother, except for a frayed safety rope.

They never found her body. The Coast Guard guys said that was not unusual. The ocean is a big place.

So is space, a voice in my head said.

Somewhere, very, very far away, a mother and father wondered what had become of their children.

For a long time, I made up stories about how my mom had survived. Maybe on a desert island or something. But I'm a realistic person, I guess. After a while I accepted it.

And after a while, Ax's parents would accept that he and his brother, Prince Elfangor, would not be returning. That they had been lost forever in space.

Lost fighting to protect Earth. To help the human race.

To help me.

I spotted Cassie up ahead, walking with some of her friends. She smiled vaguely when she saw me. We were supposed to kind of ignore each other in school, so no one ever figured out that Jake and me and Cassie and Rachel were hanging out a lot.

As I brushed past her I muttered, "Tell Jake I'll do it."

Sometimes I really hate having a conscience.

CHAPTER 11

"I wonder why these people moved?" Cassie said.

"Maybe they didn't like living next door to a Controller who is part of a conspiracy to take over the world," I said. "Or else maybe they just don't like assistant principals. I could understand that."

We were standing in the backyard of the house next to Chapman's. It was empty. There was a "For Sale" sign in the front yard. It did make you kind of wonder why these people had decided to move. Not that Chapman ever acted strange. That's the big problem with Controllers — you can never tell who is or who isn't.

"It's convenient for us, anyway," Jake said.

It was night. The moon was high and full and

bright, so we were hiding beneath a tree. There was a high wooden fence between us and Chapman's.

Ax was just changing from his human morph back into his Andalite body.

We had already acquired some ants earlier, at Cassie's barn. We were getting ready to do it. I was scared. Badly scared.

I guess the others were, too. Everyone was talking too much, the way you do when you're nervous. Cassie was shivering like she was cold, only it was about seventy degrees out.

"Tobias?" I asked. He was in the tree, just a few inches over my head on a low branch. "How well can you see?"

<I think I'll be able to see you as long as you stay aboveground,> he said. <The moonlight helps. But I'm not nearly as good at night as I am during the day. My eyes aren't much better than yours in the dark.>

"Swell," I said.

Jake glanced at his watch. "It's time. We know Chapman will be at the meeting of The Sharing, starting about now."

The Sharing is a "front" organization for Controllers. It's a way for Controllers to get together without anyone being suspicious. Supposedly, it's just a sort of combined Boy Scouts and Girl

Scouts. In reality it's a way for the Controllers to recruit willing hosts.

Yes, believe it or not, some people *choose* to accept Yeerk control.

We didn't have to ask how Jake knew about the meeting of The Sharing. Jake's brother, Tom, is one of them. A Controller who is very into The Sharing.

"You ready, Ax?" Jake asked. The Andalite had to be back in Andalite form before he could morph. Just like all of us had to be human before morphing into another being. Once Cassie had tried morphing straight from one animal to another. Nothing had happened. And Cassie is the best morpher.

<I am ready,> Ax said.

"Everyone ready?" Jake asked.

"Yep," Rachel said.

Even she sounded tense. There was a bad feeling hanging over this whole thing. Or maybe I was just being paranoid.

"Okay," Jake said. "Soon as we're all morphed, we head across the grass, down along the wall, underground. We find a crack or a hole, and enter the basement."

"Yeah. Nothing to it," I said.

I concentrated on the ant I had acquired earlier. There wasn't much to think about, really.

When I'd held the ant in my hand it had just been this tiny little dot. You could see that it had a sectioned body and legs, but that was about it.

The morphing began very quickly.

"Whoa!"

Falling! Falling!

That was the first sensation. I was shrinking rapidly. The ground was rushing up at me. It was like one of those nightmares where you are falling and falling but never seem to hit the ground.

I was still maybe a foot tall when my skin seemed to turn crisp, as if it had been burned. It became hard. Harder than fingernails and glossy black.

I looked over at Cassie and nearly screamed.

She was farther along than me. Only a foot tall and hard-shelled black all over. Glistening, ridged, plastic-looking skin.

Her legs were shriveling rapidly. So were her arms, although they had become longer, to match her legs.

The third set of legs was growing out of her chest.

And her face . . .

Her face was no longer human. Her head was sort of teardrop-shaped. Wickedly-curved mandibles were growing out of her mouth — huge, slashing, deadly-looking serrated jaws.

Her eyes had gone flat and dead. Just black dots. Antennae, looking almost like another set of legs, sprouted from her forehead.

Her waist was pinched tight. Her lower body swelled till it looked as big as a watermelon.

I didn't want to watch. Because I knew that all these same changes were happening to me. I knew it. I didn't want to think about it. I just wanted it to be over. I wanted the changes to be done.

Suddenly, all around me, huge, raspy spears shot up out of the ground!

Grass! I was diminishing to true insect size. The rough, sharp shafts that were rising all around me were just blades of grass. They weren't growing. I was shrinking.

One exploded directly under me. I tumbled, end over end.

And then my eyesight failed. My eyes simply stopped functioning.

I was blind!

Blind, and falling, rolling, cartwheeling down the side of a blade of grass.

CHAPTER 12

I was standing upright. I knew that. I had stopped falling.

But I was blind.

No, not completely blind. It was not just blackness. But my eyes saw no detail. I could see patches of light and areas of darkness. But they were misty and fragmented, and my ant brain was not interested in them.

No. The world was not about sight anymore.

It was all . . . something else. I knew I was getting something. Something . . . a sense. A feeling, almost.

Then, I could feel . . . I could feel my antennae waving. Waving back and forth, searching. Searching . . . no. They were *smelling.*

My antennae were smelling. I was looking for a scent. Several scents. It was not like human smell. Not like Jake had described dog scent when he'd morphed his dog Homer.

That kind of scent is full of possibilities. Subtleties.

This was different. I was looking for just a few scents. Just a few smells.

I tried to prepare myself. I had been through this before. There is usually a time, a brief few seconds, before the animal mind appears with all its fear and hunger and intensity. I needed to be prepared. Ants were tiny and weak. Surely their fear would be extreme. I would have to be —

Then, wham!

The ant's mind erupted inside my own!

There was no fear. None.

There was no hunger.

There was no . . . no *self.* No *me.*

No me.

No . . .

My antennae swept the air. Strange. Not home. Not the colony.

Enemy territory.

Smell them. Smell their droppings. Smell the acrid odors they smeared along the ground to mark their boundaries.

<How are you guys doing? It's Tobias. How are you guys doing?>

Strangers. The smell of others. They would come. There would be killing.

Killing. Soon.

Move.

<Jake. Marco. Rachel. Cassie. Answer me. It's Tobias. Talk to me.>

I began moving. My six legs picked their way nimbly. I was a nearly blind insect, picking his way through a forest of giant saw-edged grass blades.

Food. The smell of food. Find it. Take it. Return to the colony with it.

Change direction instantly. Move toward the smell of dead beetle. Others around. Us. Ours. They had the right smell. They were not enemy.

<You guys are heading the wrong way.>

Moving faster now. Feet feeling each blade of grass. Antennae sweeping the air, searching for the scent of the enemy. Searching for the scent of the dead carcass that we had to find and return to the colony.

<Listen to me! You are going the wrong way! The ant minds are controlling you!>

Close now. The scent of food was stronger.

Mandibles working. We would touch the carcass. We would judge its size. If it was too big to carry, we would hack it into smaller pieces and carry the chunks to the colony.

<You have to take control! You have to fight! You have to get a grip!>

Or enemies would come. And kill.

The smell of enemies was everywhere.

There. We had reached the dead beetle. I scented the air. I touched it with my legs, touching again and again to learn the size.

I? *My* legs?

Confusion.

<Fight! Fight it! You have to get control!>

It was big.

The others were with me. I opened my cutting mandibles wide and bit into the beetle, slicing tough shell, biting into meat.

<Listen to me. You are losing. You have to fight!>

Fight?

Suddenly, I realized that there had been something . . . a sound. Yes, not a smell. Not a smell. Not a feel.

<You are humans! You are *humans*! Listen to me. You are not ants. Fight it! *Fight it*!>

Yes, not a smell or a feel. In my head.

My.

Me.

Marco.

<AHHH!> I screamed inside my own head. Tobias said later that it scared him half to death. He thought I was being killed.

That wasn't it at all. I had been reborn.

<AHHHH! AHHHH! AHHHHH!>

<What's the matter?> Tobias cried.

<I . . . I . . . I lost myself,> I said. <I was gone. I was lost. I didn't even *exist.*>

<Get out of that morph!> Tobias said.

But I could hear the others now, snapping back into reality. Becoming again. Crying.

<What kind of creatures are these?> It was Ax. He sounded terrified. *Terrified.* <They have no self! I was lost! There was nothing to hold onto. They are not *whole.* They are only parts, like cells. Just pieces. What kind of foul creatures are these?>

<Listen. You guys morph back,> Tobias said. <This sucks. This isn't right.>

<Hive,> Cassie said, sounding shattered. <They are social insects. Part of a colony. A hive. I should have guessed. I should have *known.* Ax is right. Each of us is only a part. Like a single cell within a human body.>

<Guys? I see other ants. They're coming your way,> Tobias said.

<How far away?> Jake asked. <Can you see them up there?>

<I'm not in the tree. I'm right here. I'm standing right over you. You're only a few inches from my right talon.>

<I don't want to have to do this all over,> Rachel said. <Let's do this. Let's get it *done.*>

<Are we all in control now?> Jake asked.

One by one, we said yes. It was only partly true. Yes, I had gained control over the ant mind. But it was still there. It was powerful in a totally new way. It was the simplicity that made it hard. The ant was a piece of a computer. Just a tiny switch, a part of a much bigger creature — the colony.

<Guys?> Cassie's "voice" in my head. <If you try, you can kind of use these ant eyes — a little, anyway. If you concentrate you can notice light and dark. It's like watching a really, really bad black-and-white TV that's almost all snow. And you can only see what's right in front of you. But you can almost see a picture.>

She was right. I could kind of see. But nothing I saw made any sense, anyway. I could recognize blades of grass. But a long, sloped wall that seemed about six feet high was a mystery to me.

<Someone just ran over my talon,> Tobias said.

The wall. Tobias's talon.

<That's good. You're heading in the right direction,> Tobias said. <You're coming up on the fence.>

If there was a fence, you couldn't prove it by

me. I saw nothing. The bottom of the fence was seven or eight body lengths above me. Irrelevant.

<I don't want to go into Chapman's yard,> Tobias said. <It would look fishy if anyone saw. Just keep going in the same direction.>

We did. I barreled through a forest of grass. Then, very suddenly, it ended. We were out of the grass and racing across a moonscape of boulders, each the size of my head.

In my ant brain the alarm bells were still ringing. Enemies! Enemies! Their scent was everywhere.

But it was not fear I felt from the ant brain. It was not capable of emotion, or anything like emotion. It simply knew that there were enemies close by.

And it knew that it would come down, sooner or later, to kill, or be killed.

CHAPTER 13

We hit the wall. I knew it was the concrete wall of the foundation. I knew, logically, that just a foot or so over my head, the wall became wood siding. But I could not see that kind of distance.

What I saw and felt and "smelled" was that the horizontal world had simply stopped. Reality had a corner. The entire world, as far as I was concerned, was a corner between concrete and sand, one vertical, one horizontal. The concrete was full of cracks and pits big enough for me to climb inside of.

<Head down,> Jake reminded us. <Look for a way to follow the wall down.>

<There's a tunnel here,> Rachel said. <But it . . . smells . . . bad. Real bad.>

She was right. I found the tunnel, too. It was one of *theirs.* It belonged to the enemy.

<I know there is an enemy. I can sense it,> Ax said. <But who? What?>

<I don't know,> Jake said grimly. <Let's just hope they're not around.>

We headed down the tunnel. The smell of the enemy was powerful. Their stench wrapped around us. We were an invading force. We were going deep, deep into enemy territory.

The tunnel was narrow. Boulders brushed constantly against my abdomen. My legs kicked some away. Others had to be moved aside. I should have felt cramped and claustrophobic, with the earth all around me, and my friends close ahead and behind me. But my ant mind was at home in tunnels.

I was traveling down. I knew my head was pointed down, but gravity seemed less important than it did when I was human.

<There's a side tunnel up here,> Rachel said. She was in the lead. Big surprise. <There are a couple of side tunnels. It's starting to branch out. Should I YAHHHH!>

<What? What?>

<Oh, oh, oh. An ant!>

<What? Rachel!>

<He's running! He's running away. It's okay.

It's okay. He was smaller than me. He ran off down a side tunnel.>

<I guess we're the baddest ants in the tunnel,> I said, trying to joke away the sudden clutch of very human terror.

<Let's hope so,> Jake said.

<I feel air,> Ax reported. <A breeze. Down this next side tunnel.>

<Follow it,> Jake said.

Quickly we were out of the sand boulders and in a canyon. That's what it seemed like, anyway. Like a deep, deep canyon. A crack in the concrete foundation.

We clambered over craggy rocks and squeezed along the narrow crack. All the while the breeze grew stronger.

Then we were out of the canyon. We were on a flat, vertical plane.

<I think we're there,> Cassie suggested. <I sense open space all around. Air. And it's dark.>

<Okay. Morph out. But be careful.>

<Wait! Get horizontal first,> I said. <Humans can't cling to walls, and we don't know how high up we are.>

<Marco's right. And someone should go first.>

<For once, I volunteer,> I said. I couldn't wait to get out of that ant body.

First I moved away from them. It was totally

dark, so I didn't have to watch the changes in myself. But trust me, feeling them was bad enough.

Once I was human again, I began to look for a light. Then I froze.

My huge, human feet could crush my friends!

I stood perfectly still and ran my hands along the wall. Nothing. Nothing. A bulletin board. A desk! Phone. Some kind of machine, probably a fax. There! A lamp!

The sudden light was blinding. I blinked and covered my eyes with my hand. As soon as I could see, I looked around. I was in a very small room, like a windowless office. I was alone.

Then I looked down at my body. Arms. Legs. Feet. Yes! Human! Completely human.

<We see light,> Jake said. <I know you can't thought-speak now, so, if it's safe, flick the light.>

I could see them now. Four tiny ants, huddled against the corner of the wall. It took my breath away.

Had that been me? I had been one of them? Down there?

I flicked the light. Seconds later, they began to demorph. I turned away, and focused on rifling the desk.

"That was gross beyond belief," Cassie said. She was the first to complete her change.

"Yeah," I agreed.

"I don't want to do that again," she said. I could hear the shiver of fear and disgust in her voice.

I didn't answer. I was too scared to want to talk about it. If I talked about it, it would become real, you know? Better not to think. Better to shove it out of my mind.

"This is the place," Rachel said when she had grown eyes and a mouth again. "I recognize it. Chapman's office. I was a cat when I was in here, but this is it."

"Let's get this done. In and out," Jake said nervously. "Ax? Find that transponder."

Ax, now fully Andalite again, immediately began removing a panel from the thing I thought was a fax machine.

I continued looking through Chapman's desk. Nothing much there. No papers. No files.

Ax looked at me and smiled in that way Andalites have of smiling with just their eyes. He touched a small cube I thought was a paperweight. The paperweight lit up and projected a picture into the air in front of me.

"Cool," I said. "A computer, right?"

<Yes. A computer.>

I poked the air, pointing at a symbol that looked like it would be a folder. It opened. The document was written in some totally alien alphabet.

<You can use a computer?>

"Sure. Why not? This is a few hundred years more advanced than ours but —"

<Stop!> Ax said suddenly. <Go back to that last document.>

"You can read this stuff?"

<Yes.> He stared intently. <It is an announcement. The Yeerks have an important visitor arriving soon. Visser One.>

"Visser One? That would be like Visser Three's boss?"

<Yes. Visser One is more powerful than Visser Three. Just as Visser Three is more powerful than Visser Four. There are forty-seven Vissers in the Yeerk empire. Or so we believe.>

"Great," I said. "Forty-seven. Not all like our friend Visser Three, I hope."

Ax was back at work getting the transponder out of the faxlike machine. <No,> he answered. <Only Visser Three has an Andalite body. Only he can morph. Visser One has a *human* body, I believe. Ah. Here, I have it.>

He held up a tiny, shiny disk. No bigger than a pea.

"Okay, let's get out of here," Jake said. "Put that thing near the crack. We won't have to carry it as far. Everyone, morph back. Let's bail."

It was the moment I dreaded. I didn't want to return to that ant body. It made me want to cry, just thinking of it. But there was no other way. If we tried to sneak out of the basement by going up through the house, we might be caught.

"Boy, I don't want to do this," I muttered. But at the same time, I focused on that ant shape. And as I watched, my friends began to change.

Once we had shrunk back to ant size, the transponder seemed enormous. It was far bigger than we were. Standing beside it, feeling it with my legs and antennae, it felt about as big as a two-car garage.

<Everybody says ants are incredibly strong for their size,> Cassie pointed out. <Let's see if that's true.>

It seemed impossible, but Cassie, Rachel and Ax managed to lift that monstrous load off the ground.

I mean, it was like seeing three people walking down the street carrying a city bus. That's how big it was. But it's true what they say about ants. For their size, they are some strong little bugs.

When we reached the vertical wall, the three of them had to push it ahead and roll it up the wall, like some gigantic steel donut.

We reached the crack. They shoved the transponder in. Jake and I were in the lead.

It took all five of us to drag that thing over the crags of the concrete canyon. But we made it

through and back to the dirt tunnel. The transponder was so big it blocked the tunnel. It was like a spitwad in a straw. But with Ax, Rachel and Cassie behind pushing, and Jake and I clearing boulders — grains of sand — out of the way, we made progress.

It happened suddenly.

There was no warning.

One second the tunnel ahead of me was empty. The next second it was full.

Full of a charging, racing army of ants.

Enemies, my ant brain said.

Now the killing would begin.

CHAPTER 14

<They're behind us!> It was Rachel, yelling.

<Breaking through the side of the tunnel!> Cassie screamed.

<They're everywhere!>

<Help! Help!>

<Arrrrgggghhhh!>

The speed of the attack was incredible. The force of the attack was impossible to explain. There were hundreds of them. Ahead. Behind. Flooding up from side tunnels. Bursting from the walls.

<My leg! They bit off my leg!>

<Oh, oh, oh! My neck. Oh, help me!>

There were three of them on me. They were

pulling me, trying to force me down so they could tear me apart.

Tear me apart!

A fourth scampered over my head, brushing my antennae. He locked his mandibles on my narrow waist. He was trying to bite me in half.

There was no defense. We could not win. We would all be dead in a few seconds.

They were machines. Absolutely without fear. Unstoppable.

<Morph!> I yelled. <It's the only way! Morph!>

One of my legs came loose, torn away. Ripped out by the roots.

<Aaarrrgghhh!>

<No! No! Help me!>

I could feel my waist being sawed through by grinding sharp mandibles.

A searing liquid was fired at me. Poison. They were stinging me. Stinging me again and again, and ripping me apart.

Human. I wanted to be human again. Please, just let me live long enough to become human again!

<Morph!> Jake's voice. Then, <Aaaaahhhhh! No! NO!>

My waist would snap. The mandibles would not release me.

Then, suddenly, the pressure around my waist

was gone. Instead, I felt the sandy soil pressing against me.

I was growing!

I couldn't breathe. Sand blocked the air. Pressure. Then, the ground around me opened up. I swear it was like climbing up out of a grave. The air! Fresh, clean night air!

I exploded up out of the sand.

Jake was on top of me, pushing against me as he grew. And the others, who had been only inches away in the tunnel, also pressed together in a rapidly growing heap of misshapen bodies. I tried to squirm away, but it was awkward. I was only half human.

But at last I lay there on the ground, staring up through human eyes at the stars.

<Are you guys okay?> It was Tobias.

"Cassie?" Jake asked.

"I'm okay," Cassie said.

"Me, too, Jake, thanks for asking," Rachel said.

We were all alive. All in one piece. Four humans and an Andalite.

I looked down and saw the disturbed sand, where we had pushed our way up and out. Thousands of ants, almost too small to see, were racing wildly around.

There, too, in the dirt, was the transponder. I picked it up.

Rachel was stomping the ground back down, trying to flatten it out so it wouldn't look strange.

"Jake?" I said. "Let's not do this again any time soon."

He nodded shakily.

"One day I'm a lobster. Then I'm an ant. I figure the next step down the evolutionary ladder is a virus or something. And I just want to say right now, I'm not doing it. I am not going to become phlegm, even to save the world."

It wasn't much of a joke, but there was a kind of lame little laugh from everyone. And Rachel stopped stomping the ants — I mean, the ground.

That night, when I went home, I took a shower. I found the head of an ant. It was still locked onto the skin of my waist.

Lots of people think only humans fight wars. That only humans are murderous. Let me tell you something — compared to ants, human beings are full of nothing but peace, love, and understanding.

A month or so after the experience with the ants, I picked up a book about ants. The author said, "If ants had nuclear weapons they would probably end the world in a week."

He's wrong. It wouldn't take them that long.

CHAPTER 15

I was cool. I was fine. I slept okay. There were dreams, but I just put them out of my mind.

When I got up the next morning, I ignored the fact that my dad's eyes were red, like he'd been crying. He was getting worse, not better, as we got closer to Sunday. To the second year anniversary of my mom's death.

But I had to put that out of my mind, too. I had to put a lot of things out of my mind. It was getting to be a habit.

I saw Jake in the hallway at school. I pretended not to notice him.

I saw Rachel, too. She had a dark look in her eyes. Like she hadn't slept. Like something was *really* wrong.

Even Cassie seemed grim. It had gotten to all of us. It's not so easy to just forget terror. It's not easy to just ignore the memory of your leg being ripped off.

Of being dismembered. Torn apart.

One of these days, I thought, one of us is going to go crazy. Totally, lock-me-up-in-a-rubber-room nutso. It was too much. This wasn't how life was supposed to be.

One of us would snap. One of us would lose it. It could happen, even to strong people.

I knew. It had happened to my father. I used to think nothing could ever destroy him. But my mom's death had.

He used to be an engineer. A scientist, really. He's incredibly smart. We had a nice house. We had a nice car. I used to live practically next door to Jake.

I know all that stuff isn't important. I know having things isn't what life is about. But it was still hard when my dad just stopped going to work. Jerry, his boss, tried to be nice. He gave him a couple of weeks to deal with losing Mom.

But a couple of weeks was not enough.

My dad's a janitor now. Part-time. He gets jobs with a temporary service. He unpacks boxes at department stores. That kind of thing. But I don't care what kind of job he has. That doesn't matter.

What matters is that when I lost my mom, I lost my dad, too.

See, people can snap. People can lose it. I know.

I cruised through the morning classes. No big deal.

At lunch I ended up at a table with Rachel. She didn't seem to notice me. She was just hunched over her meal, eating mechanically.

A girl named Jessica came walking past with her tray. She bumped into Rachel, which made Rachel drop her fork. It splattered down in the food on her tray.

I don't know if Jessica did it deliberately or not. She's the kind of girl who thinks she's tough.

"Watch it!" Rachel snapped.

"What?" Jessica demanded, acting outraged. "Are you yelling at me? Don't give me any of your mouth, I might have to slap it for you." Then she shoved against Rachel's back.

In a flash Rachel was up, out of her seat. She spun around. She grabbed Jessica by the collar of her sweatshirt and pushed the girl back against the next table.

Jessica probably outweighs Rachel by fifty pounds. But it didn't matter. Rachel had her on her back, on the table, scattering dishes and food everywhere. Rachel leaned over Jessica and in a voice of cold steel, said, "Don't. Touch. Me."

I saw Jake across the room. Too far away to intervene. Cassie was with him. It was up to me.

I jumped up and raced to Rachel. I took a deep breath and shoved both my arms between them.

"Back off, Marco," Rachel said.

"Get her off me! She's crazy!" Jessica cried.

I pushed against Rachel, trying to force her off Jessica. Suddenly, Jessica started lashing out. I assume she was trying to hit Rachel.

She missed.

"Ow!" I grabbed my left eye. "What are you hitting *me* for?"

And that's when the first teacher showed up.

Five minutes later, Jessica, Rachel and I were sitting in the assistant principal's office.

Chapman's office.

Jessica was acting outraged in a very loud voice. Rachel was staring stonily ahead. I was wondering whether my eye would just keep swelling up.

Chapman glared at us. "What is the meaning of this?" he demanded. "Fighting in the lunchroom? And you, Rachel, of all people!"

"What, like you think she's better than me?" Jessica demanded.

Chapman ignored her. He focused on Rachel. "Is something the matter? Mr. Halloram says *you* started the fight. Are you okay, Rachel? Is there some kind of stress in your life?"

For a split second, I was afraid. The look in Rachel's eyes was dangerous. I had this terrible flash of her saying, "Yeah, Mr. Chapman, I am a little stressed. I nearly got killed turning into an ant to sneak into your basement to fight you and the rest of your evil Yeerk friends."

I knew Rachel was too cool for anything like that. But then, I would have said she was too cool to start a fight in the lunchroom.

"It's my fault, Mr. Chapman," I said.

"*Your* fault?" His eyes narrowed.

"Yes, sir. Um, they were fighting over me. See, they both want me. They're both madly in love with me, and I can certainly understand why. Can't you?"

"Are you crazy, you little toad?!" Jessica shrieked.

But when I glanced over at Rachel I saw just the slightest little tugging at the corner of her mouth. The beginnings of a smile.

Chapman yelled at us for a few minutes and told us all to make appointments with the school counselor. Then he let us go.

In the hallway outside his office, Rachel walked with me.

"I wish I could do that," she said.

"What?"

"Always think things are funny. It's why you're so . . . you know, cool and in control."

"Me? Cool and in control?" The idea surprised me. Rachel thought I was in control?

"Yesterday . . . last night . . . it got to me," she said. She shrugged. Then she smiled her supermodel smile at me. "You grind my nerves sometimes, Marco, always joking the way you do. But keep it up, okay? We need a sense of humor."

"Humor? You thought I was kidding? You mean, you and Jessica aren't both insanely in love with me?"

"Dream on, Marco," she said.

CHAPTER 16

Ax finished building his distress beacon. He had it ready the next day, now that he had the Z-Space transponder.

Now we just had to figure out where to lay our trap. It couldn't be any place that would ever be connected with us. Not Cassie's farm, or the nearby woods. Not even anywhere in town, if we could help it.

A couple days after the ant episode, we hooked up again in the fields of Cassie's farm, up against the trees of the forest. This was one area we definitely had to keep safe. It was the only place we had to keep Ax if this mission to help him escape failed.

It was Tobias who came up with the answer.

<There's a gravel quarry. It's further inland. There's never anyone there. And it is just about an hour's flying time away.>

"If we're flying somewhere we'll have to get Ax a bird morph of some type," Jake said. He looked at Cassie.

"We have a few choices in the barn," she said. She bit her lip, thinking. "We have a northern harrier that was poisoned. About your size, Tobias."

"Ax? Do you mind picking up a bird morph?" Jake asked.

<I have admired Tobias's shape. It is truly wonderful in every way. The sharp talons. The beak. Much better than the human body. Not that I mean to offend. It is just that humans have no natural weapons. I miss my tail when I am in human morph.>

"No offense taken," I said. "But you're wrong about humans having no natural weapons. You marinate human feet in a pair of old tennis shoes for a few hours on a hot day and you'll see a deadly weapon. The dreaded stink-foot."

"Okay. That's settled," Jake said. "Now, let's get down to details. If we're going to call down a Bug fighter we need to have a plan ready. Saturday should be the day, I think."

"As long as it doesn't involve ants," I said. I meant it as a joke. But no one laughed.

"No ants," Jake agreed quietly.

I shook my head in amusement. "You know, we're talking about taking on Hork-Bajir and Taxxons. I used to think they were the scariest things in the world. But it's the little ant that scares me worst now."

When the meeting broke up I hung around till Jake was done saying good-bye to Cassie.

Jake and I walked home together. For a while we talked about the normal kinds of things we used to talk about before. Before our lives changed.

We talked about basketball and disagreed over which was the best NBA team. We talked about music. Neither of us had bought a new CD recently. We even talked about whether Spiderman could kick Batman's butt or vice versa.

You know, stupid, normal, everyday stuff.

I was stalling because I didn't want to have to tell him what I had decided.

But Jake's been my friend forever. He knows me.

"Marco? What's the problem?"

"What do you mean?"

"I mean, you haven't said a single mean-

yet-funny thing the whole way. That's not you."

I laughed. Then, I just blurted it out. "This is my last time," I said.

"What do you mean?"

He knew exactly what I meant, of course. "I'm in for this time, but that's it. No more after that. And I'm serious. No one is going to 'guilt' me into it. I've done enough."

He thought about that for a while as we walked. "You're right. You have done enough. You've done a million times more than 'enough.' "

"It's just been too many close calls."

"Yeah."

"One of these days we aren't going to pull it off, you know? Ten more seconds and those ants would have had us. And before that it was a pot of boiling water. And before that I was practically killed by sharks. I mean, come on. Enough is enough."

"You're right," Jake said.

"Yeah."

I was surprised that he took it so well. I guess I shouldn't have been. We all kind of treat Jake like he's the leader, but he's never been pushy about it.

"What are you going to do Sunday?" he asked.

That took me by surprise again. "I don't know. Some Sundays we go to my mom's grave. Leave flowers and all. But this is the two-year thing." I shrugged. "I don't know, man."

He just nodded.

"But I'll tell you one thing, Jake. A year from now I don't want my dad going to leave flowers at *two* graves."

CHAPTER 17

<This is wonderful! Wonderful! Flying!>

The six of us were all together. Flying. It was the first time for Ax. He just kept saying how wonderful it was. He wouldn't shut up. It was the most excited he'd been since he'd discovered coffee.

Which was cool, because flying really *is* wonderful.

<These are excellent eyes!> Ax said. <Far better than your human eyes. Even better than my Andalite eyes.>

<Yes, birds of prey usually have great daytime vision,> Tobias said. <I think mine may actually be a little better than yours, though.>

<I doubt that,> Ax said. <It is hard to imagine better vision than this.>

<Remember the good old days?> I asked. <When we used to argue over who had the best jump shot? Now it's who has the best bird eyes.>

We were sailing above a patch of woods. It was almost solid green below us. We had risen high on a beautiful thermal. A thermal is a warm bubble of air that acts like an elevator, letting you soar high with almost no effort.

We hoped there were no bird-watchers down in the woods. We made a very unlikely flock — a red-tailed hawk, a falcon, a harrier, a bald eagle, and two ospreys. We kept some distance between us so it wouldn't be too obvious that we were together.

Also, the eagle, who was Rachel, was carrying something that looked like a small TV remote control. She was the biggest bird. She got stuck lifting the weight.

<I have an idea,> I said. <Let's just blow off this suicide mission and spend the day flying around.>

<Sounds good to me,> Cassie said. She meant it to be lighthearted. It sounded just a little too serious.

<There's the quarry,> Tobias announced. <Dead ahead.>

<Dead ahead. Excellent choice of words,> I said.

We made a large circle over the area, looking for anyone who might be in the woods. But there was no one.

We spiraled down from the sky. Down into the deep, open gash in the earth that was the gravel quarry. It was a desolate place. Just a big hole in the ground with some water in the lowest spots.

A few minutes later we were back in our usual forms. Minus shoes, of course. And wearing our motley collection of morphing clothes.

"We look like a trapeze act from a cheap circus," I said. "Way too much Spandex."

"Don't start with the uniforms again," Rachel said.

It was an old debate. I would say how we needed some decent superhero uniforms. You know, like the X-Men or whatever.

But now, I realized, I shouldn't be talking that way. As if we were all going to be together in the future.

I couldn't tell if Jake had told any of the others that I was quitting. Probably he had told Cassie. I doubted Rachel knew, or she would have said something. The same with Tobias.

And Ax? Who knew with Ax? He was still a mystery to us. It was one of the things I would miss after I quit. I mean, how often do you get to hang out with a real alien?

That and the flying. I would miss the flying. But if I was out, I had to be out all the way.

I guess I must have looked morose, sitting there on a pile of rocks, thinking. Jake came over and kind of gave me a shove. You know, in a friendly way.

"Come on. We need to go back under that overhang. Out of sight."

"Great," I said. "The rocks will fall and crush us and we won't have to worry about the Yeerks."

There was a sort of shallow cave in the quarry wall. Not deep at all, but it would hide us from anyone flying over.

"Well," Jake said. "Let's try this out. Ax? You ready to trigger that thing?"

<Yes. I am very ready, Prince Jake.>

Jake looked around at everyone. "You all ready to go into your various morphs?"

We nodded. All except Ax. See, we were all going to go into morph — our strongest, deadliest morphs — in order to take care of the Yeerk crew when they came. But Ax didn't have anything but a shark, a lobster, an ant, and a harrier. We figured he was better off in his own Andalite body, which was plenty dangerous.

"Okay, Ax? Do it. Everyone? Morph!"

"And let's keep our fingers crossed," I added. "Or talons, claws, or hooves, as the case may be."

Ax pressed a button on the distress beacon. As far as we could tell, nothing happened.

<It is working,> he reassured us.

So, Rachel, Cassie, Jake, and I began to morph. These were all morphs we had done before. There would be no battle to maintain control over the animal mind.

Rachel went into her elephant morph. We figured we might need that brute strength and size.

Jake slowly became a tiger. Cassie used her wolf morph. And I focused on my gorilla.

"What a freak scene this is." I laughed as the changes began. "Anyone who stumbled onto this would think he'd lost his mind."

It was definitely odd. You haven't seen weird till you've seen pretty, blond supermodel Rachel grow a trunk as thick as a small tree and ears the size of umbrellas.

Or Cassie, growing gray fur over every inch of her body, falling to all fours and baring long yellow teeth.

And then there was Jake. Huge, curved claws grew from his fingers. A snakelike tail whipped out behind him. Orange and black fur covered him. And when he was done he was a full grown tiger. Almost ten feet from his nose to his tail. Easily four hundred pounds.

If something deadly can ever be beautiful, it's a tiger.

<Bet I could kick your butt,> I said to Jake.

<Yeah, monkey boy? I don't *think* so.>

<Hey, I could stomp both of you,> Rachel said. She walked closer, swinging her trunk and flaring her ears out. A moving mountain.

<This is *so* mature,> Cassie said. <Arguing over who could beat who.>

<Hah. You're only saying that because we can all kick your butt, wolfie,> I pointed out.

<As if!> Cassie protested. <You'd have to catch me first. And I could still be running long after the three of you were worn out and fast asleep.>

<You have an amazing variety of animals on your planet,> Ax said. <Some day, when the Yeerks are defeated, Andalites will come here simply to try out the many animal forms. It would be like a vacation.>

<Joe Andalite, you've won the Superbowl! Now where are you going?> I said, mimicking the Disney World commercials. <I'm going to Earth to turn into a lobster!>

<I don't understand,> Ax said.

I started to explain, but just then a red light

began to flash on Ax's homemade distress beacon. <The response signal! They are coming!>

<Quick! Everyone to your places!> Jake said.

He slunk away, liquid power, to hide in the shadow of a boulder. Rachel pressed back under the shallow overhang. Cassie trotted to a spot to the right of Jake, and I tried not to look like a four-hundred-pound gorilla behind a pile of gravel. Tobias flapped hard, struggling to gain altitude.

SWOOSH!

It came in low, just above tree level, then disappeared before turning to come back.

A Bug fighter. Just as we'd planned.

<Here's your ride home, Ax,> I said.

CHAPTER 18

Swoosh!

The Bug fighter flew over once again, seemed to pause, then settled down toward the floor of the quarry.

Bug fighters are the smallest of the Yeerk ships. They aren't much bigger than a school bus. They have a cowled, insectlike look, except that on either side there are very long, serrated spears pointing forward. So they look a little like a cockroach holding two spears.

The Bug fighter landed as gently as a feather.

I held my breath.

<Wait for it,> Jake said. <Wait for it.>

The hatch opened. Out stepped a Hork-Bajir Controller.

The Andalite prince, Ax's brother, had told us that the Hork-Bajir were a good, decent people who had been enslaved against their will by the Yeerks.

Uh-huh. Maybe so. But what they looked like was a whole different thing. Hork-Bajir are big, walking razor blades. They're about seven feet tall, two arms, two legs, and a nasty spiked tail similar to Andalite tails.

There are swordlike blades raked forward from their snake heads. There are blades at their elbows and wrists and knees.

I mean, let me put it this way: If Klingons were real, they would be scared of Hork-Bajir.

<Get ready.> Jake again.

The Hork-Bajir stepped clear of the Bug fighter. Then, he just stood there.

<There will be a Taxxon inside,> Ax reminded us.

<Yeah. We know,> I said.

Why was the Hork-Bajir just standing there? He should be looking around. After all, he was answering a distress beacon. Why was he just standing there like he was waiting for something?

<On the count of three,> Jake said in our heads. <One . . . Two . . . Three!>

"Tsseeeeerrrr!"

Tobias swooped, falling from the sky at close

to a hundred miles an hour. He raked his talons forward and hit the Hork-Bajir's face.

"RROOWWWRR!" Jake leaped from cover. He sailed through the air and hit the Hork-Bajir with paws outstretched, claws bared.

The Hork-Bajir went down hard.

Jake rolled away as the Hork-Bajir slashed the air like an out-of-control Cuisinart.

But just then Rachel rumbled up, as big as a tank.

<Okay, back off, Jake,> Rachel said. <I have him.>

She pressed one big, tree-stump leg on the Hork-Bajir's chest and pressed him down against the ground. She did not crush him, just held him like a bug who could easily be squashed.

The Hork-Bajir decided it was time to stop struggling and lie very still.

Too easy, a part of my mind warned me. *Too easy. No Hork-Bajir Controller had ever just given up like that.*

But I had other problems. My job was to get inside the Bug fighter. Get the Taxxon pilot.

<Let's go!> I yelled.

I ran forward, loping clumsily on my squat gorilla legs, swinging my massive, mighty gorilla arms. Cassie and Ax were right there with me. Taxxons are disgusting, oversized centipedes, but

I wasn't worried. We were more than enough to handle a Taxxon.

But then —

Zzzzzzzzaaapppp!

A brilliant red beam of light sliced the air just inches in front of me. It blocked my way.

Zzzzzzzzaaaapppp!

Another beam of blinding red light. This crossed behind me. It exploded gravel into steam as it traced a path!

<Dracon beams!> Ax cried.

I spun around, looking for cover.

Zzzzzzaaaaapppp!

<Look!> Cassie screamed in our heads. <Up on the edge of the quarry!>

I looked, as the dracon beams formed a cage of deadly light around us. The edge of the quarry above was lined with Hork-Bajir. I looked left. More! To the right . . . more!

The entire quarry was lined with Hork-Bajir warriors, each armed with a Dracon beam. There must have been a hundred of them. We were surrounded.

Completely surrounded.

<Stay in morph,> Jake snapped. <Don't let them know we're human.>

<Let's charge them!> Rachel yelled.

<No! You can't even climb up that rock face. Don't be stupid!>

Cassie called Tobias. <Tobias! You can get away!>

<I don't think so,> he said. <No headwind. It would take me a couple of minutes to flap my way up out of here. They'd fry me before I got clear.>

The reality settled over us. The despair.

<What are we going to do?> Cassie wailed.

<There has to be a way out! There *has* to be!> Rachel yelled.

<Not this time,> I said grimly.

We were trapped. Outnumbered. Outsmarted.

Finished.

And that was when *he* came.

CHAPTER 19

He looked so much like Ax. So much like Prince Elfangor. And yet, so totally different. The difference wasn't something you saw. It was something you felt.

A shadow on your soul. A darkness that blotted out the light of the sun. Evil. Destruction.

Not the impersonal, programmed destructiveness of the ants. This was warm-blooded, deliberate evil.

His body was an Andalite. He was the only Andalite-Controller in existence. The only Yeerk ever to infest an Andalite body. The only Yeerk with the Andalite power to morph.

Visser Three.

Visser Three, who had murdered the Andalite Prince Elfangor while we cowered in terror.

Visser Three, who even the Hork-Bajir and Taxxons feared.

<Well, well,> he said, thought-speaking to us. <I have you at last, my brave Andalite bandits. Fools. Do you think we never change our frequencies?>

<*Yeerk!*> Ax said in a silent voice loaded with hatred.

Visser Three's main eyes focused on Ax. <A little one,> he said, surprised. <Are the Andalites now reduced to using their children to fight?>

Ax started to say something, but Jake snapped, <Shut up, Ax! None of us communicates with *him*. Give him nothing.>

Ax fell silent, but he was practically vibrating with rage and hatred for the Yeerk Visser. It wasn't surprising. Visser Three had killed his brother.

But Jake was right. We couldn't get into a conversation with Visser Three. The rest of us still wanted to hide the fact that we were humans, not Andalites. We could too easily slip and reveal the truth.

Visser Three seemed to be enjoying his big moment. <What a colorful assortment of morphs,> he said. <Earth has such wonderful animals, don't you agree? When we have enslaved the hu-

mans and made this planet over in *our* image, we will have to be sure and keep some of these forms alive. It would be entertaining to try some of these morphs myself.>

None of us said anything. At least not anything that was human. Jake did snarl, drawing his tiger lip back over his teeth.

<Especially you,> Visser Three said to Jake. <That is a beautiful, deadly animal. I approve. In fact, I was going to demand you demorph. But I have a better idea. You see, we have a guest aboard the mother ship. It will be entertaining to show you to Visser One as you are.>

I was sick with dread and fear. But not so afraid that I didn't notice a sneer in Visser Three's tone when he said "Visser One."

<Did you catch that?> Jake asked me in the thought-speak version of a whisper.

<Yeah. Visser Three doesn't like Visser One.>

Visser Three must have given some signal, because at that moment his Blade ship appeared overhead, shimmering into view as it decloaked.

The Blade ship is far larger than the Bug fighters, and very different. It is jet-black. It's built like some kind of battle-ax from the middle ages, with two curved ax-head wings, and a long, diamond-pointed "handle" aimed forward.

<We're better off making a run for it!> Rachel said.

<It would be suicide,> I said. <As long as we're alive, there's hope.>

<Yeah. Visser Three is taking us to the Yeerk mother ship to show off for his boss. Some hope.>

But Rachel did nothing. And I did nothing. And we all just stood there, under the watchful eyes of a hundred Hork-Bajir.

They must have landed out of sight while we were busy watching the one Bug fighter.

Ax had used the wrong frequency. The Yeerks had figured out we were laying a trap. And our trap had become Visser Three's trap.

A couple of dozen of the Hork-Bajir leaped down from the high wall of the quarry and surrounded us. They kept their Dracon beams leveled at us as the Blade ship landed on the quarry floor.

"Go, obey *farghurrash* there *horlit*!" one of the Hork-Bajir said, in the strange mix of English and their own language that they use.

He pointed to the Blade ship. A door had opened in the side.

<I can't fit in there,> Rachel said.

But as she approached the door, the door widened to her size. It stretched and grew as if the metal skin of the Blade ship were alive.

What a pathetic little crew we were, trooping inside the Blade ship. Weak and pathetic and

stupid to imagine that we could ever have resisted the Yeerks.

Visser Three was right. We were fools.

This wasn't even my fight, I thought. Not really. This wasn't my time to die.

I guess I wanted to feel angry. But what I felt was numb, as I trooped into the Blade ship with the others. You know, like I wasn't really there, almost. I was past feeling anything, I guess. I just kept thinking, *It's happening. It's finally really happening.*

The next day was Sunday. My dad would go to my mom's grave. Alone.

It would be a while before he would admit that I, too, was gone.

Just like when my mom died — there would never be a body.

Just like my mom.

CHAPTER 20

<This is not looking good,> I said. I couldn't take the silence anymore.

<No. It isn't. But we're not dead yet,> Jake answered.

<Yet. Why doesn't that make me happy?> I asked. I looked around at the others, all crammed into a windowless steel cube. Black, dimly lit steel walls on all six sides. No door. It was like a coffin.

<We look like some kind of circus,> I said. <An elephant, a tiger, a gorilla, a wolf, and a freak of nature.>

That got some halfhearted laughs from the others. I don't know why I was making jokes. I guess that's the way I am. When bad things hap-

pen, I tell jokes. But inside I felt sick. Like I had swallowed broken glass.

<Maybe we should just demorph,> Cassie said. <Maybe if they realize we aren't Andalites, they'll let us go.>

She knew that was dumb, of course. But when you're scared, you start grabbing at anything. You want to believe there's a way out.

The truth was, there were exactly two possibilities. Visser Three would kill us. Or Visser Three would turn us into Controllers. He would infest us with a Yeerk.

<We should stay in animal morph,> Jake said. <I mean, the thing is, if Visser Three learns we are human, he may go after our families next. He may figure we told them something.>

<Prince Jake is right,> Ax said. <The Yeerks will not want to take any chances that other humans know of them.>

It was true. I knew it was true. I guess I'd known it all along. But hearing it said, it made me want to crawl into a corner.

My dad. Cassie's parents. Rachel's mom and her sisters. Jake's parents. Maybe even Jake's brother, Tom, although he was one of *them.* Their lives were at risk, too.

Suddenly, a window opened in one of the walls. It just grew, the same way the door had before. Like the steel was alive. It formed a round porthole, large enough for all of us to see — even Rachel, who could only turn her massive head enough to look with one eye.

I gasped.

Below us, blue and white and so beautiful it brought tears to your eyes, was Earth.

Sun sparkled off the ocean. Clouds swirled over the Gulf of Mexico, a big spiral, maybe a hurricane.

<Look,> Cassie said simply.

We looked. Through the eyes of the animals of Earth, but with the minds of human beings, we looked down at our planet.

Our planet.

For now, at least. For a little while longer.

Then something different came into view, as the Blade ship rotated away from Earth.

<This is why the Yeerks opened a window,> Ax said. <This is what they wanted us to see. So that we would despair.>

The mother ship.

It was a gigantic, three-legged insect. The center was a single, bloated sphere. The sphere was flatter on the bottom, and from the bottom hung a weird, mismatched series of tendrils. Like the tendrils of a jellyfish. Each one must have been a quarter-mile long.

Around the sphere were three legs, bent up, then back down, exactly like a spider's legs.

<The legs are the engines,> Ax explained. <The tendrils hanging down below the belly are weapons and sensors and energy collectors. That is also where the shipboard Kandrona is. The Yeerks must bathe in the Yeerk pool every three days and absorb Kandrona rays. There must be one on the planet below, too.>

<Yeah. We know,> I said. <Your brother told us. For all the good it did us.>

It just hung in orbit, like a predator gazing down hungrily at blue Earth below.

<I can't believe people on Earth don't see this on radar,> Rachel said. <I mean, it's huge. It's a city!>

<It is shielded,> Ax said simply. <It cannot be seen by radar. And it would normally be invisible to us. Visser Three is showing it to us. To terrify us.>

<He's doing a good job,> I said.

<I've never been in space before,> Cassie said. <I always wished I could. I always wanted to see Earth, all in one piece like that.>

<It is a lovely planet,> Ax said gently. <Not so different from mine. Except that we have less ocean and more grassland. I . . . I am sorry I brought you all to this. This is my fault.>

I wanted to yell, "Yes! Yes, it is your fault!"

But Cassie said what we all knew in our hearts. <Ax, you're only here because your peo-

ple wanted to protect us. Your brother and a lot of Andalites died trying to save us. Nothing is your fault.>

It was true. But sometimes, when everything hits the fan, you don't want the truth. You just want someone to blame. <One too many missions,> I muttered. <This was going to be my last one. Now . . . well, it will still be my last one.>

I could see an opening in the side of the Yeerk mother ship — a docking port. As I watched, a pair of quick Bug fighters flew in, dwarfed by the size of the opening.

A minute later, we entered the docking port and were suddenly bathed in deep red light.

Through the window, we could see Yeerk crewmen — Hork-Bajir, Taxxons, and two or three other alien species, in simple red or dark brown uniforms. And there were humans, too. My first reaction was hope. Humans!

But then I realized the truth. No. Human-Controllers. Yeerks. No different than the Hork-Bajir.

There was a slight shudder as the Blade ship came to a halt.

<Ax?> Jake asked. <What's our morph time?>

<We have been in morph for forty percent of allowable time.>

I did the math. <So we've used up forty-eight minutes. Leaving what, seventy-two minutes?>

<Yeah,> Tobias confirmed. <Not a lot of time for you guys. Maybe Rachel is right. Maybe we should just go out in a blaze of glory. Attack as soon as they open the door. At least we can let them know we were here.>

I saw Jake extend his claws, as if he were thinking about using them. He glanced at where the door had once been, like he was measuring the distance. I knew that he was listening to the tiger in his head.

Then he seemed to relax. <No,> he said. <We have to have hope.>

Cassie sidled up next to him and nuzzled him with her wolf's muzzle.

I guess it should have been funny. The wolf and the tiger, sharing a tender moment. But all it did was make me a little jealous. They had each other.

<We gave them a pretty good fight, didn't we?> I said. <Our little circus? We did some damage to them.>

<Yes, we did,> Rachel agreed.

<Do . . .> Ax hesitated. Then, <Do humans fear death?>

<Yes. We're not crazy about death,> I answered. <How about Andalites?>

<We're also not crazy about it.>

Through the window we could see a lot of

Hork-Bajir and Taxxons and humans running around, racing to get somewhere. They were lining up. And now, I noticed, there were distinct kinds of uniforms, one red-and-black, the other gold-and-black. The brown uniforms were all around the edges, like they were less important.

Suddenly, without warning, the window stretched open into a large, arched doorway. Fetid air rushed in, smelling of oil and chemicals and something else.

A ramp rose up from the steel floor outside to meet us. We were standing like a display at the top of the ramp. All around, filling this side of the docking bay, were uniformed Hork-Bajir, Taxxons, and humans. Most were in red-and-black. Perhaps two hundred creatures, standing in stiff rows, arranged by species.

About a quarter of the total were in gold-and-black. There were more humans in this group, but also some unusually massive Hork-Bajir.

<Jake? I have a feeling. I don't think the reds like the golds.>

<I think they are troops of two different Vissers,> Ax said. <I . . . I think I overheard my brother talk about that. Each Visser has his own private army in their own uniforms.>

<Swell. I wonder which group gets to have us?> I said.

Far at the back of the rows of alien troops, there was a movement. A party of creatures walking to the front.

Visser Three was at the center, followed by two big Hork-Bajir in red.

And just to his left was a human. A human woman with dark hair and very dark eyes.

That was when I stopped breathing. Because I knew. Even before I could see her face clearly. I knew.

They marched up to the bottom of the ramp. A dozen soldiers leveled Dracon beams at us, just in case we wanted any trouble.

Then, in thought-speak that all could hear, Visser Three turned to the woman beside him. <You see, Visser One. I have taken the Andalite bandits. The crisis is over. Your trip here is wasted, and you can return to the home world.>

Visser One nodded. She looked up at us with those dark brown, human eyes.

Eyes I knew. Eyes I remembered.

The same eyes that watched me sleep every night from the framed picture beside my bed.

My mother.

Visser One.

CHAPTER 21

I sat down. Very suddenly. I'm sure it looked funny. A big, hairy gorilla simply falling down.

I would have laughed if I'd seen it.

My mother. Not dead.

Alive!

I wanted to yell. "Mom! Mom! It's me, Marco!"

But Jake was in my head, a loud, urgent whisper. <Marco? Don't say anything. Don't do anything. Do you hear me?>

So I wasn't just imagining it. Jake had recognized her, too.

<Marco? Listen to me, man. You have to hold it together.>

My mother . . . alive.

My mom.

<Come on, Marco, stand up. Don't make them suspicious.> He was speaking just to me.

I could hear Jake. I could. But it seemed to come from far off. He didn't understand. It was my *mom*. My mom!

<Marco? That is not your mother. Not anymore. That is *not* her.>

<Jake? It's my mom. Look, it's her.>

<No, it isn't, Marco. Not anymore. They have her. She's one of them. One of *them*!>

<Why, Visser One,> Visser Three sneered, <you seem to have frightened the humanoid one.>

"It is called a gorilla," Visser One said coldly. "If you are going to be in charge of Earth, Visser Three, you should at least learn something about the planet."

<And take a human host body, like you did? No, I think not. Human bodies are weak. I much prefer this Andalite host.>

My mother looked at him and curled her lip. "I took a human host and learned about the planet and the humans. And because of that I was able to begin the invasion that you have now endangered with your criminal incompetence!"

Visser Three's deadly Andalite tail twitched, as if he was going to stab my mom . . . Visser One. The red troops tensed up. The gold troops let their hands edge toward their weapons.

<Ooookay,> Rachel said. <I think we were right. These two definitely don't like each other.>

She didn't know, I realized slowly. Rachel didn't know. But she had never met my mother. Neither had Cassie or Tobias. And Jake had kept our talk private.

Visser Three slowly relaxed. <You would *like* to provoke me, Visser One,> he said. <But the fact is that I destroyed the Andalite force. I shot down their dome ship. I killed Prince Elfangor myself and heard his dying screams. And now I have eliminated this last, pathetic rabble of Andalites.>

My mom . . . Visser One . . . just smiled. "You want to be Visser One? You think you can take my title? We shall see. The Council of Thirteen does not like Vissers who make mistakes. And you have made mistakes. Be careful of your own ambition."

She snapped her fingers, and every one of the soldiers in gold turned. Then she walked away, followed by her gold-uniformed troops.

That was not my mother. At least not the creature who called herself Visser One.

Visser One was the Yeerk inside my mother's brain.

But the sickening thing is, you see, that the host mind is still alive. It is still aware. Some-

where inside that head, behind those painfully familiar eyes, my mother still lived.

<Take it easy, Marco,> Jake said. <I know how it is. I know how much you want to do something. But now is not the time. They'd cut us down before we got two steps.>

<I know,> I said dully. I hated myself for not trying, but I knew there was nothing I could do. I had to hide inside my morph. Never let my mother know it was me. Never let her know . . .

Slowly, heavily, I stood up. I felt weak. A very strange feeling for a gorilla.

I think right then, if I had been in any other morph I would have just surrendered and let the animal mind take over. Let instinct rule, and wash away my human emotion.

But the gorilla was too much like a human. Its instincts were gentle. Like humans, it was a creature with emotions. It could not protect me from the pain.

<Don't tell the others, Jake,> I said. <You're the only one who recognized her.>

<Okay, Marco.>

<You can't even tell Cassie, okay?>

<It's okay, man. You are my oldest and best friend. You know that. No one will ever know from me.>

Visser Three still stared at us. I think he wasn't sure what to do next.

<Six Andalites,> he said. <Six Andalite bodies that could be used by my most loyal lieutenants.>

Ax exploded. <And then there would be others like you, you filth! Other Andalite-Controllers. More unnatural abominations like your vile self!>

Visser Three cocked his head thoughtfully. <Why are you the only one who speaks? You're right of course: Why would I allow anyone to acquire Andalite morphing powers? But you are a child. Why do the others remain silent? And why do you all still hide in your morphs? Curious. Very curious.>

He seemed to think it over for a minute. Would he realize the truth? Would he figure out that the reason we remained silent was so he wouldn't guess that we were human? Would he figure out that's why we stayed in morph?

He seemed to shrug.

<Take them back to a holding cell. Triple the guard. If there is the slightest trouble, kill them all.>

CHAPTER 22

They marched us down a hallway. Rachel, still in her huge elephant body, filled the hallway like our ant bodies had filled the tunnels in the sand. Tobias rode on my shoulder, unable to fly in the cramped space.

The place we ended up was just like the bare, black-steel prison we'd been held in on the Blade ship. But this time no window appeared.

There was dim light that seemed to radiate from the ceiling. But nothing else at all.

I slumped down in a corner.

<What's our time look like, Ax?> Jake asked.

<You have only thirty percent of your time left.>

<Thirty-six minutes,> Jake translated.

<Thirty-six minutes and I'll spend the rest of my life as an elephant,> Rachel said. <Not that the 'rest of my life' is likely to be much time.>

For a while everyone talked about various plans for escape. It was all just talk. We knew we were trapped. We knew it was over. We were aboard the Yeerk mother ship. It was huge. If we had a week to learn our way around, we'd still have been lost in its maze.

There were hundreds, probably thousands of armed Yeerks — Hork-Bajir, Taxxons, and a few other shapes we'd never seen before, and of course, humans.

Like my mother.

My mother — Visser One. Most powerful of the Vissers.

When had it happened? Had the Yeerks taken her much earlier? Had she already been a Controller for those last years when she was with us? When she had come to my bedroom to say good night, had that been a Yeerk slug, just playing a part, like an actor?

When I tried to fake sick to get out of school, had it been a Yeerk who saw through my story and kidded and joked me into admitting it?

Was it a Yeerk, handing out the presents on Christmas morning? A Yeerk, singing in the

church choir? A Yeerk, pulling the puppet strings of my mother's body when she dragged me through J. C. Penney's and made me buy school clothes I didn't really like?

Was it a Yeerk I used to find making out with my dad like a teenager when they didn't think I saw them?

All of it an act? All of it fake? For how many years?

How much of what I'd thought was my mother, had been . . . one of *them*?

One thing was sure. Her death had been faked. The so-called drowning accident. No body recovered.

But the body *had* been recovered, hadn't it? The Yeerks' mission had been accomplished. The invasion of Earth had been started. Visser One was leaving Earth in the hands of Visser Three. And so she had to disappear and not leave anyone asking questions.

<There has to be *something* we can do!> Rachel was saying.

Ax said, <My people have a saying — grace is the acceptance of the inevitable.>

<Yeah?> I said suddenly. <Well, I don't *accept.* That's what *they* want. They want the entire human race to lie down and accept the inevitable.>

Jake turned his big, yellow tiger eyes on me. I saw Tobias's eternally fierce glare.

I stood up.

<I have a saying for you. I got it from a fortune cookie. 'Fall down seven times, get up eight.' You know what that means? That means you don't ever just lie there. You always get up. You always come back for more. You never surrender. Maybe you die, but you never surrender.>

They were all looking at me now. Through the eyes of a wolf and a hawk and the big, sad eyes of an elephant.

<Ants,> I said. <We can morph to ants again.>

Cassie was shocked. <You're saying that? You? I thought you hated those ant morphs as much as I did.>

<I did. But it may work. We morph to ants. Maybe there's a crack here somewhere. We escape into the walls and the machines. We can hide, then morph into something more dangerous, attack, and then disappear again. Maybe even find a way to destroy the Kandrona.>

<That's nuts,> Rachel said. <I like it.>

<At least we can hurt them a little before they catch up with us,> Jake agreed cautiously. <Except for Tobias.>

<You have to do what's right for the group,> Tobias said. <I'll have to take my chances. I'd

feel better knowing you guys were still out there somewhere, making trouble for the Yeerks.>

<It may work,> Ax said. <The Yeerks are not very familiar with morphing, except for Visser Three. They may not expect an insect morph.>

<All right, then,> Jake said. <Let's —>

The door opened. It simply appeared silently in the wall.

Standing there were three Hork-Bajir. They were wearing gold uniforms.

Lying on the floor were four other Hork-Bajir. They were each uniformed in red. They were either dead or unconscious.

<Don't move,> Jake snapped as he saw Rachel and me tensing up for a charge.

The lead Hork-Bajir, a huge creature maybe eight feet tall with head blades that were more than a foot long, eyed us.

He spoke. It was surprising, because he did not speak the usual strange mishmash of languages the Hork-Bajir used. This one sounded like he'd been educated at Harvard.

"This hallway goes on in that direction for a hundred feet." He pointed to his left. "Then comes a guard station, where there will be two Hork-Bajir and a Taxxon. From there, four hallways. Take the one furthest to your left. Follow it to a dropshaft. Take the dropshaft down fifteen decks. Directly ahead you will see escape pods."

He looked at Rachel. "You are too large in that morph to fit in the escape pod. You will need to demorph when you get there. The pod is programmed to return you to the planet in the same area where you were seized. The pod will then self-destruct. Do you understand?"

We all just stared.

<It's a trap,> Tobias said.

<No. We're already trapped. They could kill us any time,> I said.

<Marco's right,> Jake said. <Why let us escape if they want to kill us?>

<This is one of Visser One's soldiers,> Ax pointed out. <It would be very embarrassing for Visser Three if his prisoners should escape, no?>

<Politics,> Cassie said, with a laugh. <It's about politics! Visser One is making Visser Three look bad. If we escape, it will be blamed on Visser Three.>

"You will have to deal with any of Visser Three's troops you encounter between here and the escape pod," the gold-clad Hork-Bajir said. "Leave. Now."

<Ax?> Jake asked.

<Only fifteen percent of your morph time is left.>

<That's about eighteen minutes. Let's do it!>

Visser One's troops turned and marched away.

<I'll go in front,> Rachel said.

<Okay. And let's move,> Jake said.

Rachel squeezed her massive tonnage into the hallway. <All right. Now let's see who wants to try and stop me!>

CHAPTER 23

Whomp! Whomp! Whomp! Whomp!

Rachel made the steel floor vibrate with each massive step. Her leathery sides scraped the corridor walls so that I could only catch occasional glimpses past her.

The hallway was empty until we reached the guard station. Just as the Hork-Bajir had said.

Rachel didn't even slow down.

Whomp! Whomp! Whomp! Whomp!

I saw a flash of a Taxxon, foolishly running as if to cut her off. A few seconds later I had to jump over the crushed remnants of the big centipede.

<Look out! Hork-Bajir!> Cassie yelled.

He exploded out of a side corridor, a red-uniformed Hork-Bajir.

Swooosh!

A razor-bladed arm sliced the air inches in front of my face.

<More coming!> Tobias warned. <Both directions! All of them in red!>

<I can't turn around!> Rachel moaned. She was too big, too tight a fit in the corridors to turn and help, as half a dozen Hork-Bajir in Visser Three's livery came screaming onto the scene.

<I knew it couldn't be that easy,> I said.

<Battle!> Ax said, sounding like he was announcing a party.

I felt the same way. I was ready. I was mad and tired of feeling helpless.

The closest Hork-Bajir swung at me again and sliced a six-inch long cut in the matted fur of my huge shoulders.

That was all it took. Like I said, gorillas are peaceful, almost gentle creatures.

But don't go making one angry. Especially not when a boy who wants very badly to hurt some Yeerks is sharing space in the gorilla's head.

"Hoohoo hoo hhawwwrr!" I cried and swung a fist the size of a cinderblock into the stomach of the Hork-Bajir. I gave it all I had. I put every ounce of the gorilla's muscle into the blow.

The Hork-Bajir was lifted clear up off the deck. His head slammed the ceiling. He was down and out of the game.

Out of the corner of my eye I saw another Hork-Bajir leap at Ax. The Andalite's tail flashed forward so fast you didn't even see it move. The Hork-Bajir staggered back, minus an arm.

<Good one, Ax!>

<You as well! Hah hah!>

I decided right then — I kind of liked Ax.

<Rachel!> Jake yelled. <Keep moving. Left tunnel. Look for a dropshaft, whatever that is. The longer we stay here, the more of these guys are going to show up.>

Just then, right on cue, two more Hork-Bajir came up from behind us. <You guys move! I'll deal with them,> Jake said.

The Hork-Bajir rushed us.

"RRRRRRROOOOOWWWRRR!"

Jake let loose with a roar that must have been heard from one end of the mother ship to the other. It even scared me. And it sure made the Hork-Bajir hesitate.

He was on them, while they were still thinking about what to do next.

Hork-Bajir are very fast. But so are tigers.

One Hork-Bajir was down, with Jake sinking fangs into his snakelike neck. The other Hork-Bajir looked around to make sure no one could see him, then decided he'd like to live. He kept his distance.

Jake backed away but kept his face turned to

the Hork-Bajir behind us. We trotted as fast as we could down the hallway, now a scene of devastation.

It was like the ant tunnels. We could only try to escape. The longer we tried to fight, the more the odds would turn against us.

Suddenly . . .

<Ahhhhhhh!>

<Rachel!> I heard Tobias cry.

<It's okay. I found the dropshaft. I am . . . dropping.>

<What is it?> I asked.

<An elevator without a floor,> Rachel answered.

Then I was there, at the edge of a long shaft that went down and down, maybe forever. Rachel already looked small. Which was not easy for her to do.

<He said to stop after fifteen levels!> I reminded her.

<Yeah? And how do I do that?>

<Think the number! It hears speech and understands simple thought-speak commands,> Ax instructed. Then added, <At least that's how it works on *our* ships.>

<I'm slowing down. Cool!>

<More Hork-Bajir back here! And some of those other ones. The little wrinkled ones!> Cassie yelled. <They're coming fast!>

<Here goes nothing,> I said. I took a look down the dropshaft and jumped off into empty space.

You know, if it hadn't been for the fact that I was just a few minutes from being trapped forever in a morph, and if there weren't a dozen or so walking Salad Shooters after me, it would have been fun.

I fell, but not too fast.

<Fifteen levels,> I thought as floors zipped past me.

Twelve levels down, I plummeted past a human Controller who was getting ready to step into the dropshaft. He had a very human look of total amazement on his face. Possibly because while standing there, he'd seen a flying elephant, followed by a gorilla, a wolf, an Andalite, and a tiger.

<Hork-Bajir, coming fast!> Tobias warned.

I looked up the shaft. A big Hork-Bajir warrior was gaining on us. But there was nothing I could do until he reached us.

<He's mine,> Tobias said. He flared his wings, flapped hard and was shooting back up the dropshaft toward the falling Hork-Bajir.

"Tseeeeer!"

Tobias's talons came forward, outstretched, and slashed the alien's eyes.

"Ghaahharrr!"

The Hork-Bajir clutched at his face. I guess

he was too distracted to think about what floor he was heading to. He shot past us as we slowed to step onto the fifteenth level.

Hard floor under my feet again! A very good feeling.

<Rachel! You have to demorph!> I reminded her.

<Already working on it,> she said.

She was shrinking even as she lumbered along.

<The escape pods! Ahead there!> Ax cried.

They were only a dozen feet from us. A few seconds more and we would make it.

Rachel stumbled. She was half-human, half-elephant. A nightmare of pink and gray, with huge ears and human hair and fat arms and legs that had no feet.

I reached down and swept her up with my powerful arms. She was still large, maybe three hundred pounds. But not too much for me to carry.

We reached the door of the escape pod.

It closed behind us as we wedged our oversized bodies inside.

<Ax! Time!> Jake yelled.

<Five percent of the time remains!>

<Six minutes. Morph out!>

There was a surge as the escape pod ejected from the underside of the Yeerk ship.

My dense black fur was already starting to disappear by the time the pod rotated. I could see Earth below.

Earth.

And as the tiny ship turned, I could see the Yeerk mother ship.

It was kind of a joke now, I thought. The Yeerk mother ship. My mother on the Yeerk mother ship.

Hah hah.

Before I became fully human again, before I lost the ability to thought-speak and had to return to words spoken out loud, I said, <Jake?>

<Yeah, Marco.>

<No one ever finds out. No one can ever know.>

<Okay, Marco,> he said.

<My mother died two years ago tomorrow.>

<That's how it will be, my friend.>

<Yeah. But someday . . .> Someday, somehow, in some way that I could not foresee, we would win this battle. Humans and Andalites together would defeat the Yeerks. And we would free all of their slaves.

All of them.

<Someday,> I whispered again.

<Someday, Marco,> Jake said.

CHAPTER 24

I guess there's no such thing as a nice graveyard. But the place where my mom is remembered is as nice as it can be.

The grass is green. There's a tree nearby. It's always very quiet. You can smell flowers.

I hate going there.

My dad stood for a long time, looking down at the white marble headstone. It has my mom's name. The day she was born, the day she died. And a message that says, "No wife, no mother, was ever more loved. Or more deeply missed."

My dad and I stood a few feet apart. We didn't say anything. We both just kind of cried.

You probably wouldn't think I was the kind of guy who would cry. Mostly I don't. Mostly I make jokes about things. It's better to laugh than to cry, don't you think?

I do.

Even when the world is scary and sad. Especially when the world is scary and sad. That's when you need to laugh.

"Two years," my dad said. It surprised me.

"Yeah," I said. "Two years."

He took a deep breath. Like it was hard for him to breathe. "I . . . I . . . look, Marco, I've been thinking."

"Yes?"

"I haven't been a very good father to you." It wasn't a question, so I didn't say anything.

"Your mom . . ." He had to stop for a moment to get his voice under control. "Your mom would not be happy about the way I've been these last two years."

What could I say? I decided to say nothing.

"Anyway. I talked to Jerry the other day."

Jerry was his old boss. Back when he had a regular job.

My dad shrugged. "I guess we have to live, huh? I mean, we can't . . . you know." Another heavy breath. "Your mom wouldn't want us to give up, would she? Anyway, I'm going in Monday to talk to Jerry about getting back to work. You know . . . see if I still remember how to even turn on a computer."

It was a big thing. A big decision. I guess what I should have done was run over to give him a hug and tell him I was proud of him. I *was* proud of him. But that's not me.

"Oh, Dad, you never could figure computers out. Especially games."

He stared at me with the blank eyes I had seen for the last two years. Then, suddenly, he laughed.

"You punk kid, I've forgotten more about computers than you ever knew."

"Oh, right! So why did I always kick your butt whenever we played Doom?"

"I *let* you win."

I made an extremely rude noise. "Yeah? How about if we just go home and play a game so I can show you how totally wrong you are?"

I couldn't stop him from giving me a hug. I guess I didn't mind all that much.

We walked away from my mother's gravestone. The stone that marked the death of a woman who was not dead.

I raised my eyes up to the sky. The blue sky of Earth. My home.

She was probably gone from the mother ship, now. Off to some other corner of the galaxy.

But wherever she was, no matter how far, I would find her.

Someday . . .

Don't miss

#6 The Capture

"My . . . head . . ." I said.

<Headache? No surprise, dude.>

"Something . . . wrong . . . I can't . . . think."

<Don't worry. Take a break. We have it under control. More or less.>

<Unbelievable,> said a voice in my head. <Can it be? *Humans?*>

What was that voice? Where was it coming from?

Marco lifted me and slung me over a horse's back. Cassie.

<Cassie? A human, yes. And Rachel? The cousin? Human as well?>

. . . What was happening? There was a voice inside my head.

We were running now, running and running at full gallop, through trees, across lawns, down suburban streets where Cassie's hooves clattered loudly.

We jumped a fence. I flew through the air and landed hard on the dirt.

I felt pain, but it came from far away.

. . . I looked around. Trees, everywhere. A panting horse standing nearby.

I saw all this, but in a distant way, as if I were watching it all on TV. My eyes moved left, right. They moved all on their own. Like someone else was focusing them.

Cassie. I tried to say her name. Cassie.

But no sound came from my mouth.

<Don't struggle, Jake,> a voice in my head said. <It's pointless.>

What? Who was saying that? What was . . . ?

Then, a laugh that only I could hear. <Put that primitive human brain to work, Jake. Jake the Animorph,> it sneered. <Jake, the servant of the Andalite filth!>

Then I knew.

I knew what the voice was.

A Yeerk!

A Yeerk in my own head.

I was a Controller. . . .